Whispers in the Shadows

A Horror Anthology

The display type was set in Goudy Bookletter 1911.
The text type was set in Garamond.

Published by Rowanwood Publishing, LLC.
www.rowanwoodpublishing.com

First Edition

Introduction

We are the Just-Us League, a group of friends dedicated to the craft of telling stories.

We come from all over the world. We all have different backgrounds and different styles of writing. But we all have storytelling in common. We bonded over our writing, and our love of putting words onto a page to entertain is what makes us truly happy.

For our third anthology, we have chosen a darker theme— that of horror, the kind that creeps up behind you in the night (or stalks you by day). From the deepest shadows of our imagination, we have conjured ten original horror stories. A living reflection, a killer on the loose, a cruel magic ritual, and many more terrors lurk within. Some are magical, some are supernatural, and some are a little bit too real. Turn the pages and discover a cat lady's ultimate sacrifice, the dangers of the doldrums, and a mysterious beast that craves its murderous yearly hunt.

Without further ado, we present to you the *Just-Us League Anthology: Volume Three*. Please enjoy. And leave the lights on when you read…just in case.

Sincerely,
The Just-Us League

Table of Contents

The Cat Lady

Louise Ross

James clung to the recliner arm, digging his fingers into the padding. The stuffing had fallen out and the mechanism was broken, so the whole thing sank back to one corner and kept him at a cock-eye angle.

A tabby cat sat straight as an Egyptian statue in the corner, glaring at him. Same cat in the same place like every visit. That constant stare set his nerves on edge.

The recliner was a trap, and if that cat attacked, he'd never be able to scramble out in time to protect himself. They didn't offer a cat self-defense class at school and between student council and school-mandated community service hours, he wouldn't have taken it anyway.

Two cats circled him, cutting between him and Mary. Another cat lay over Mary's shoulder and studied him. James scrunched back into his chair. Plan B, he'd pull the floppy recliner cushions around him as a shield. The cats creeped him out.

The springs creaked as he shifted, and all four cats noticed. The two circling cats moved a paw's width closer to him. They'd established some kind of patrol and every movement threatened the demilitarized safe zone he occupied. The inquisition vibe made it hard to concentrate on Mary's stories, not that any of the stories were new but— she was a nice old lady and he was there to be her companion for a few hours.

Mary's hand, skin pulled over wire fingers with marble knuckles, reached up and pet Cali, the watcher. Cali's teeth snapped at the hand, and Mary laughed as she pulled her hand away.

"She is quite in command these days." Mary pressed her hands together. A small smear of blood colored her skin.

"Let me get you a paper towel." He nodded at the blood and struggled out of the chair. A puff of old lady and dusty fabric accompanied him.

"Don't go to the trouble."

Walking into the kitchen, he spoke louder so she could hear. "No trouble at all." Any reprieve from his cat guards was worth the effort.

The kitchen was tiny. Maybe a breakfast table with two chairs could fit into it, but there was no table or old divots in the linoleum where one once sat. He suspected that when her husband was still alive, they ate in the living room. Five cabinets separated a sink and a stacked oven/microwave combo. The counters were clear of napkins, but there was a dish towel covering a pile on the floor. If there was a towel on the floor, she had to have more. He pulled open drawers looking for another towel. Two drawers of cutlery and a cabinet of glass casserole dishes later, he found a drawer with a single dish towel.

Turning, two cats sat less than an arm's length away. One's matted hair stuck up in spikes and darkened into a mud color. Their tails swished across the floor, gathering dust. Another cat, black and white like he wore a tuxedo and two white gloves, stood on the counter with his hindquarters up and his ears back. He growled. Waves of spasms squeezed James's stomach, and he took a step back for distance.

"Found a towel," James announced, hoping the cats would scatter.

They didn't, so he strode through them as fast as he dared.

They flanked him, escorting him back, like he was their prisoner or their next target.

"Thank you, James, but I got it stopped." Mary held up her hand. Other than the darkening red color, the blood had clotted. Cali hopped onto Mary's lap and pawed the hand. When Mary lowered the gnarled finger, Cali licked the dried blood. Mary laughed again. "It appears she feels bad for biting me and has decided to clean my wound. Such a good mother." Mary's fingers ruffled Cali's head as the cat continued licking the blood.

James shuddered. He would be very happy if he never had to see a cat fed human blood again!

"I wanted to thank you again for letting me come here for my community service," James repeated. His mother lectured him on how important it was to be grateful for what others did, and at least he wasn't stuck in some hospital or ladling soup somewhere. Picking up a few sticks and eating hamburgers with an old lady was way better than what some of his classmates were doing.

"No. It is a joy to have you. You are always welcome to come see me."

"Thanks. I'll come again tomorrow. Probably around five. Okay?"

"Absolutely. I'll be here waiting for you."

James nodded to the sack of uneaten hamburgers near her feet. "Should I bring something besides hamburgers? Are you worn out on them?"

Mary's grin brightened. "Oh no. These are wonderful. I appreciate them so much. You are a shining moment every time you come by, and these gifts, well, they aren't necessary, but thank you so much. My babies thank you too."

He grimaced. The idea of the cats eating the hamburgers offended him. He wasn't feeding the blood-licking troops, but if she wanted to starve herself to feed the cats, he couldn't stop her. James shrugged it off. "No problem. Is there anything else I should bring tomorrow?"

Mary shook her head. "No. Thank you, James."

"It'll be my last visit. My service hours are almost done. Is there anything you want me to do? Mow? Clean the gutters?"

Mary turned her head in the first part of a refusal and stopped. Her chin tilted to the side.

James's hopes sank. He wouldn't get a free pass and be told not to come back or to consider his hours over.

"Would you help me update my shelter list? I like to keep a list of the local shelters and who are accepting animals and which ones are the no-kill shelters."

The cats circled. The possibility of shipping the cats out to a kill shelter didn't really upset him, but even these cats deserved a chance at survival. "Yeah, I can help with that." He pulled his phone out of his pocket and waved it around. "I always got my internet on me."

"Great. Thank you."

With a few more back-and-forth gratitudes, James escaped into the late spring evening. The long sleeves of his shirt clung tight to his arms, and he pulled it off. Two hours the next night then his community service for school would be done.

***

Rain came and went overnight. Dark, wet shadows remained on the sidewalk, but that suited Mary fine. The grass looked less yellowed and the dirt less like a coming dust bowl when even the sidewalks had a shadowed, dirty demeanor. The air smelled empty and was still cool enough that she breathed easily. Raising her eyes to the lightening morning sky, she thanked the good Lord for a pleasant start to the day. It would be another long one after all.

The journey started slow. Her knees no longer bent as well as they used to, and her ankles wobbled, balancing to take the next step. None of which mattered. This would be the day everything changed.

Yanking the sleeves of Charlie's shirt over her hands, she grabbed the door handle and stepped into the First Baptist Church's Giving Center.

Toby, a pleasant middle-aged man, glanced up from his table and offered a smile, but his eyes never lifted in joy and only his sigh greeted her.

"Ms. Mary, good morning. How are the cats?"

Nodding, she met his fake smile with one of her own, but hers was honest. If nothing else, she would enjoy a moment to sit down and this bit of conversation. It could be the last time they spoke, so she'd make it the best chat they ever had.

"The babies are just fine. Mr. Whiskers has been particularly naughty recently." She chuckled, thinking of his antics. "The boys have been hunting the house, and Mr. Whiskers has discovered how to get into the upper kitchen cabinets. I came home yesterday and found him pushing the cups out."

Toby jerked his head toward a chair, and she took it. The release of pressure from her feet eased the pain. It was a moment of calm in the river of erosion that ate away at her body.

"Did he break anything?"

In fact, he had. The glittery pile of glass shards decorated her floor in a festive sparkle. The large pieces were easy enough to pick up, but the best she could do was sweep the tiny pieces into the corner. A dish towel covered the pieces when she went to bed, but this morning it was gone. The cats had probably taken it and chewed through it. She knew better than to leave things on the floor, but if they were hungry enough to eat fabric, the rest of this day would be much easier on them.

"Nothing too important. Cali has gotten very talkative recently. She has a way of cocking her head to the side. I just know she knows what I am saying, and she is not the least bit interested. I think she's telling me that my stories are old and she's heard them too many times." Mary rubbed at her knees. The ache intensified as she sat, informing her she'd been inactive too long. "If I'm not going to feed her, she's not interested in listening. She's become very watchful recently and has claimed the hall closet for herself, hissing and spitting if I get too close. I bet she's nesting again, and I'll have a litter of kittens soon."

Toby laughed, a single blast of mirth that died immediately after. Charlie used to do that. That was his signal that he hadn't heard her or that he didn't actually think her story was funny. That was fair too. She wasn't funny. Her charm centered around being positive and proactive. When things needed doing, call on Mary. Mary makes things happen. She couldn't hold her own personality against the man any more than she could fault him for doing his job.

"What are the chances of getting supplies today?" She had to ask. If she didn't ask, there would be no chance of getting what she needed.

Toby's smile sank. The frown matched his eyes. Finally, he became a solid person instead of two mismatched pieces in a puzzle game.

"Sorry, Mary. I can only give supplies out once a month. It's only been a week." The file drawer of the desk opened. His fingers flipped through and pulled a sheet of purple paper. The whole thing happened without his eyes leaving hers. In this dance of request and refusal, he performed the choreography without stumbling, and she reached out to accept the paper out of habit and practice.

The magic purple paper held no power anymore. It was a polite way to push her out the door, but it meant they cared. The church had taken considerable time to make connections and create this list. Even though he had given her this list many times in the past, he handed it over like it was the first time. Performing perfectly for his audience of one. She took it and scanned the names. None of the resources had changed in over a year, but she double-checked just in case.

"There are some good resources on that list. Maybe one of them can help you."

Smiling, she nodded. "Thank you, Toby. That's very nice." She stood. The hammer of her weight slammed down on her joints, and they screamed obscenities back at her.

She swallowed her grunt and grinned at the silly legs.

Didn't they know that any amount of whining and complaining wouldn't get them anything? No one cared for rude behavior. "I hope you have a wonderful week, Toby. May the Lord bless you, your good works, and all that the church does for the community. You all have been a godsend to this old woman."

Toby's fresh smile actually reached his eyes. "Thank you, Mary. We try our best."

Waving, she left him and the Giving Center with her purple paper in hand. It was only six blocks of good sidewalk to the Neighbor's Pantry, a program that served a single meal a day with fruit and vegetables and a main dish like a baked potato or pasta. They'd let her take hers in a to-go container, if she brought one in. Her hand reached into her pocket and crinkled the paper bag there. One good meal would pull the cats through one more day.

The sun sprinkled warmth onto her back, battling the chill in her arms. A small rock hitched a ride in her right shoe. It snuck in through the hole in her toe, wandered under her arch, and finally sat under her heel for the long run. At the bus stop, she sat on the metal bench with another woman. The lady in her suit jacket studiously avoided eye contact, but that didn't bother Mary.

"It really is a beautiful day," she told the lady as she untied her sneakers. The left side of the lace was three times the length of the right side, and she evened them out as she removed the shoe. "Nothing that happens on a day like today can be truly horrible."

"Sure. Yeah." The lady offered a half-grimace and stood.

The rock was a red-orange one. It would be at home in an Arizona desert or a decorative garden, but it didn't match the dull gray concrete of the city streets. It truly stood out, called for attention. Giving it the place of honor it deserved, Mary set it down on the ledge of the bench back. A small dot of color on a long stretch of sameness. It made her think of modern art or maybe the Japanese flag.

"Goodbye," Mary told the rock and continued on.

"Bye," the lady answered.

Mary nodded to her and hoped she had a cheery and wonderful day.

The Neighbor's Pantry was in a basement. The back stairwell of the church had broken concrete steps. A metal railing painted in a collection of red, blue, and worn-away metal helped her down the stairs. The shade kept the rail cool to her fingers, and it was solidly anchored, holding her whole weight as she took each step one at a time.

The door had a unique flair with a southwestern blue center rubbed thin on the edges, showing a salmon pink under the paint. The sunburst greeted her, inviting her into the air conditioning. Homeless and poor street people littered rows of tables with attached circle stools. A small child laughed, clapped his hands, and banged a bottle on the table. Pots clanged in the kitchen area. Warm tomato mingled with body odor.

"Hi, Stella," Mary greeted the lady standing near the kitchen.

Stella's hands splayed out on the wall behind her. Her hips bounced on and off the wall in rhythm with the bobbing of her head. White wires tracked from a single earbud down to her jeans' pocket. Her dark hair was pulled back in a ponytail, and her lime green t-shirt advertised Habitat for Humanity Build Day.

"Hello." Stella grinned.

"That is a wonderful program." Mary nodded at the shirt. Plenty of the people here in the building would need those homes.

"Would you like to know when the next one is? We always need volunteers. If nothing else, it would help to have someone bring water around or pass out sandwiches."

Mary nodded. Too bad she wouldn't be able to help. "You let me know when it is."

"Great. We have soup today. Are you eating with us?"

Mary's hope for help faltered. She couldn't carry soup home in her paper bag.

"Thanks." Mary glanced around. "But I need to get home. My cats will miss me."

"Oh." Stella's eyes grew wide. "Mr. Whiskers and Nala, right? How are they?"

If nothing else, Stella remembered the cats. "They are fine. Nala is getting the boys in control. I came home a few weeks ago, and she had the boys cornered in the bedroom. She would select one of the boys and they'd go out on patrol and come back to her. She's formed them into a true pride. My little lions. They are getting to be quite the hunters."

"Are they lion colored?"

Shaking her head, Mary scanned the room. "No, they aren't." With their fur darkening, they all were a muddy dark color. They could be turning into jaguars, but Mary wasn't sure if jaguars hunted in prides. "But what would be my chances of getting a sack lunch instead of soup?"

Stella's mouth turned down. "I don't think we have any today, but I'll ask." She edged the door open and twisted inside. "Hey, John, got any sack lunches?"

"Nah," a man answered.

"Can we make one?"

"Ain't got any bread today. Might get some later."

Stella turned back around, already mid-shrug. "Sorry. No sack lunches today, but stick around. Soup will be done soon."

The minute hand clicked past the six indicating it was half past noon. The walk to the Salvation Army would take another hour. A lunch to take home could make all the difference. Her cats needed something and soup wouldn't fit in her pockets well.

"I appreciate the offer, but I need to be moving on." Mary turned back toward the door.

"Hey," Stella called her back. "I don't have a sack lunch, but I got some crackers." Stella held out a fist of individually wrapped crackers.

"Thank you." The little packages filled her pockets and added plastic crinkles as she pulled herself up the stairs. She walked to the rhythm of her own music. As she conquered the stairwell, she turned a small victory circle to the crackling noise. The day was looking up. It wouldn't be enough, but it was a start.

***

The walk to the Salvation Army took longer than normal. Her breaths came faster and the pain in her knees and ankles kept her from taking full steps, but it gave her more time to appreciate the beauty as she walked.

The spray paint art might need a few touch ups, but the alley works ranged from artfully designed names to panoramas of cultural diversity and even one wall with a basketball game. Sugar skull reapers in black cloaks dribbled a ball down court against Globe Trotters in 50s short shorts.

Pushing through the harsh concrete, lines of clover and grass peeked up and brightened the dullness. Cars whooshed by, the lights created a low but energetic hum, snips of music rushed out as business doors opened and shut, and the outdoor patio of a coffee shop added flapping canvas when the wind caught the umbrellas. Gas fumes layered with espresso bitterness tinted the air.

Yet she felt alone.

Drivers hid behind their glass windshields, the metal patio chairs remained empty, and when she walked by the bus stop, anyone not engrossed in their phones quickly looked away. It didn't matter. Soon she'd be home, and she'd be welcome there.

The Salvation Army came into sight, and it glittered with glass like the shining beacon it was. This would be her last stop today. James promised to come by and see her in the evening. If he was kind enough to want to see an old lady, she'd be there for him too.

The Salvation Army building had fancy electronic sliding doors on the front where shoppers entered, and double glass pull doors welcomed potential workers to the occupational rehabilitation office. Mary shuffled to the side entrance and the less intimidating steel security door. It took her body weight to yank the door open. If she had the breath left after opening it, she'd laugh. Nothing was more secure than a door that didn't open, and there was a sense of security in knowing that anyone who came in behind her would make just as much noise.

The back room was the warehouse. Storage shelves climbed up to the ceiling. Big items like furniture filled the bottom area and smaller pots and pans filled the higher shelves. The section of business casual clothes sat just outside the interior door for occupational services. Four long rows of tables lined an open area. Small bags sat on the table.

The room bustled. It wasn't just Yolanda today. A group of teens in matching red shirts, saying "Feeding the Faithful," measured rice into baggies and stacked boxes of dried goods. Along one table, rows of cans were separated into corn, green beans, and pineapple chunks. They had a feast to feed the entire city for a solid meal. A man in his forties walked along the group and cheered them on.

Yolanda wasn't in the warehouse, so Mary walked along the edge, back to the office area. On the other side of a glass window, an older gentleman in a button-down shirt and trousers sat with his feet up on a chair. Mary waved at him.

His face scrunched up, and his head tilted to the side. For a moment, he was the human version of Cali. She knocked politely at the door and glanced back in the big picture window. He waved her in.

"Excuse me." Mary only half-stepped into the room to avoid bothering him too much. "Have you seen Yolanda?"

He puffed out a breath, and his feet thwapped against the concrete floor as he sat up straight. "You're looking for food."

It wasn't a question, but Mary nodded in answer. "Yes, sir. I—"

"No." He stood and held out a hand. "Yolanda no longer works here. There will be no food handouts. Go around to the career center doors. They'll help you find a job. Sustainable income." With every step, his outstretched hand pressed her out of the office doorway. He backed her out until he stood outside the door as well.

Mary opened her mouth to let him know she had an open case with the career center but that she had been turned down at her last two job interviews and was waiting for the job fair the following weekend. Before she started the explanation, he preempted her.

"Go on. It's the double glass doors on the side of the building."

Well, that was it. Nodding, she turned. Even if James brought more burgers, it may not be enough on its own. Her darlings had chewed through the burgers too quickly, devouring them. That was alright. The cats wouldn't go hungry. A soundtrack of pouring rice and chatting teens accompanied her exit. It was only a little after two. She could make it home by four and James wasn't due until five. There'd be enough time.

The walk home expanded like walking on a treadmill. Every step took her half the distance it should have. As her ankles swelled through the day, her pace slowed down. She paused on a bus stop bench to loosen her shoes. The drag of too much exercise and no water made her mind fuzzy. Between two long blinks, the shadows stretched out and the traffic picked up. Her body fought her when she stood, but she'd be home soon where she could sleep.

Her home waited for her just as she had left it. The yard hadn't become suddenly lush, but in the evening light, it reminded her of autumn. A season of change. The wind brushed across her cheek, agreeing that change was coming.

She opened the front door. The lock no longer turned, but that didn't matter. She'd sold everything of value, and the door kept her babies safe inside.

Nala greeted her first. She sat in the entryway with a straight back and watchful eyes. Only after Nala turned did Mr. Whiskers and Penguin come out. Her two boys paced in front of her.

Her hand shook as she pulled out the cracker packages. The boys would have to be happy with those, at least until after James came by. The packages ripped open, and the crackers fell out. The boys pounced on the crackers, cradling them with their paws as they licked off the salt. With the boys out of the way, Nala returned to watch. With deep wisdom and persistence, Nala tilted her head to the side, demanding the rest.

Guiltily, Mary pulled out the last cracker package, the one she hoped to save for herself, and opened it for Nala, who accepted the crackers and left.

The clock told Mary it was just after five. It wouldn't be long now. Placing a wooden kitchen chair by the front window, she sat and watched for James.

Nala kept watch at the door. Cali curled up behind her neck. The boys circled, ducking out of the way each time Mary reached down to pet them.

Six o'clock came and went without fanfare. Charlie's old wall clock with the chime was sold in the estate sale just after his death, and she missed its cheery greeting to each hour.

James didn't arrive.

The cats didn't make a fuss. Still, teenage boys weren't known for punctuality, so she kept waiting. The sun sank and darkness overtook the lawn. Distant streetlights tossed shadows into her yard, but the day was done. She was alone with her cats, and it was over. Finally.

Nala's posture and command of the others had become too apparent in the last few months, and Mary needed Nala to understand. Turning in her chair, she talked directly to Nala.

"Nala—" she kept her voice strict like she had when her sons had gotten into trouble "—this is it. I'm going to meet the Good Lord. He provides for all his creations. As He takes me into his loving arms, He will provide for you and the others. You take this gift as it was intended, freely and with love. You understand?"

Nala cocked her head. After a moment, she stretched her long body out, kneading the carpet with her paws. Then slowly, she stalked forward, head low and hindquarters high.

Mary nodded in agreement. She pulled a small pocketknife. The brushed metal casing hid a blade only one inch long. The tip was rounded from stabbing into too many tin cans and the edge wasn't sharp, but it was what she had at hand. The metal felt cool against her skin like death's embracing hand. Lifting her eyes to the ceiling, she gave one last prayer.

"Good Lord, you have provided so much. You are truly miraculous. As I come to greet you, do not abandon those I leave behind. Be with Toby and his church with their good works and help them find new resources so they can continue. Give Stella and the Habitat for Humanity group the strength of arms and knowledge to build the homes people need." Mary pushed the blade firmer against her skin, accepting the pain because life was both pain and promise. In this pain was the promise of her eternal rest.

"Help Yolanda find a new job where she can continue to help those in need. Be with the church group who is heading out to feed the faithful, and most of all, check in on James. I'm worried about him because he did not show up today." Without thinking about it, her eyes dropped from the ceiling to the window, searching for James's car one last time.

"Finally, Lord, thank you. Thank you for a little red rock that brought a touch of color in a dreary day, for your natural grace that comes through no matter how much concrete it must battle, and thank you for the sun and rain. Thank you for providing for my cats. I come to you joyfully. Amen."

***

James pulled up outside the rundown home. The light rain from the day before made the yard look like a giant mud pit with sprigs of grass. He grabbed a bag of burgers from the front seat and a bag of cat food from the back.

His mother lectured him for half an hour the night before about staying late at school for a student council meeting. Like he could change student council or skip. School was important, more important than two community service hours. It wasn't like the service hours were scheduled anyway. His mother hadn't seen it his way, so she took away two service hours from his log and made him bring the cat food.

Mary didn't come to the door when he knocked. He stood on the concrete step and waited. Two knocks later, he twisted the knob. The door opened.

Three cats ran out, and he stumbled back out of their way. "Mary?" He peeked around the door into the house. "Are you home? Sorry I missed yesterday."

Mary's shoe, a worn-out purple sneaker with holes in the sole, lay in the living room, and he stepped in to see if she was there. A cat stalked from the living room toward him. It was the black and white one. Or it had been, but the tuxedo was no longer white. A reddish-brown color coated his chest. Even his white mittens were dark. His guard patrol was clear. Bloody paw prints layered in paths. Bloody pinpoints dotted the prints.

The air James sucked in felt heavy and sticky in his lungs. "Mary? I think one of your cats may be injured? Are you here?"

Inside the front room, Mary sat in the chair, her skin torn open. Cali sat on her lap. Her head cuddled against Mary's arm, streaking red along her fur and inside her ear. Her paws clasped onto a flay of skin, and she gnawed it.

James bent over, throwing up. The psychopathic cats were eating Mary, and he'd just let half the pack out the door to hunt the neighborhood. It caused acid to boil in his stomach and burn up his throat, heaving even after his stomach was empty.

Cali hissed at him. Her mouth opened, showing two fangs.

James ran. Paws scrabbled on the entryway floor, tearing after him.

Yelling at the phone to call his mom, he drove home. In his rearview mirror, four cats ran across the street. He swerved, barely missing a parked car. Two blocks away, he caught the swish of a tail disappearing behind a house. He shivered. The whole ten blocks home, his phone rang, went to voicemail, and dialed again.

"Mom!" he shouted into the phone as he unlocked the front door and ran in. The door crashed against the wall, but it did not matter. He'd seen the cats running after him.

Mary was dead.

Eaten by killer cats.

"What?" his mom answered in stereo through the phone and from her spot on the couch.

"Mary—"

His mom turned around to face him. The news played in the background. A fire raged on screen, but it seemed so trivial compared to the horror he'd unleashed.

"Ma—" He coughed and bent over, breathing hard. His voice caught in the coughs.

"What about Mary? Why aren't you there? Didn't you promise to go see her? If you are skipping out on your service hours, I will take all of them away and you will start over w—"

"Mom!" James's voice shook. "Mary's dead."

"What?" His mom stood up and started dialing her phone.

"She's dead." The words rang out in his head, but he couldn't tell if he was screaming it or not. She wasn't just kind of dead, she was torn-to-bits, human-jerky, cat-food dead.

His mom held her phone to her ear, and he could hear the ringing on the other side. "She's not answering."

"Duh. She's dead!"

His mom gave him a stern look, but he didn't care. He hadn't meant to yell, but he was having trouble controlling himself. His arms shook, he was ten seconds from throwing up again, and he hadn't told his mom about the cats—the cats that chased him down the street.

His mom dialed a new number and put the phone on speaker.

"Emergency services. What is your emergency?"

James shut his eyes tight and opened them. The door was open. "Mom!"

"My son just found a woman dead." His mom grabbed her purse and her keys, but James was already turning to shut the door. He wasn't going back to Mary's.

In the front door, the black-and-blood-colored cat sat with its darkened chest, licking its paw white again.

"Mom!" James pointed at the black-and-blood cat.

Behind him, Cali stalked up the front path with her tail raised. Her head swung from side to side, tracking James's movements. She took slow measured steps. Her shoulder blades jabbed up above her head, accenting her plan to slice him to death. Behind her, Nala sat at the street, watching.

James ran to shut the door, but two cats jumped on him, hissing and biting. They smelled of blood and Mary's house.

He smacked at them. The large yellow cat yowled. As if it had given a command, the yellow cat and blood-colored cat separated and took position. In coordination, they leapt.

His mother screamed, and he twisted. James batted a cat away to see it leap after his mother. Kicking the door closed, he scrambled to get ahold of the attacking cat. It twisted and turned until its claws and teeth stabbed into his leg. As he ripped it away, its teeth tore his calf open. Blood welled into the tear. He opened the door long enough to throw it out.

His mother had dropped her phone.

"Please stay calm. Help is on the way," the operator told them.

His mom got ahold of her cat. Its body jerked like a snake. Her grip loosened and James clamped onto it before it escaped. He tossed it out the back door.

"What the eff!" His mother placed her back to the wall between the living room and kitchen.

"The cats killed Mary," James shouted.

"Sir, slow down. Explain from the beginning," the phone asked.

James grabbed the phone. "Mary's cats killed her, and now they are chasing me."

"Find somewhere safe and stay there. A patrol car will come by. Do you understand?"

"Yes. Hurry!" James shouted.

The call hung up.

"James." His mother's voice cracked.

James turned to face her. Out the back door, two cats crossed paths, watching the house. They'd used the same pattern at Mary's house when they stalked him into the kitchen. Back when Mary was feeding them drops of her own blood, training them to think of humans as prey.

James checked out the front window. Cali sat at the front walk, watching the door, but Nala, the watcher, turned and examined the street. Her head turned as a car rolled by.

James rushed back to the back window and his mom. "They are watching the street." He whispered it.

"Why?" His mom's pupils dilated until only an outline of color ringed the darkness.

James wanted to scream that he didn't know, but the acid in his throat and the itchy uncomfortable hours at Mary's house made him pretty sure.

"Prey."

A patrol car came down the road and blipped its siren.

The cats paused in the yard. Their ears perked up. The yellow cat's eyes flicked away. They ran.

James rushed to the front window. Cali stalked down the sidewalk after two teens holding hands. One cat waited sentinel at the edge of the lawn while the others followed Cali, weaving in and out of car tires.

XVI
THE LIGHTHOUSE

The Lighthouse

Mckayla Eaton

Morning arrived after, what seemed to Megan, the longest of nights. She'd spent the night huddled against the wall opposite her bedroom door with her pocketknife clutched in her hands, fearing that at any moment the intruder would try her door and, finding it locked, bust their way in.

But no one tried her door. All night she listened but didn't hear a sound.

Equally exhausted from fear as she was from lack of sleep, she found the nerve to leave her room. She unlocked her door and slowly pushed it open.

Sunlight streamed into the hallway, washing the faded wooden floor in a pale light.

She didn't see any blood.

Knife still in hand, Megan left her room and padded down the hall.

The interior of the lighthouse was rustic, though it had modern lighting and plumbing. It had been her father's sole project for years. He'd bought the long-retired lighthouse at a bargain price and immediately moved himself and Megan into it, selling their house and most of their possessions back in Halifax. The first winter had been cold, and Megan still remembered many nights snuggled in blankets in front of the wood stove, her father telling stories about the many lighthouse keepers who had lived in the place once upon a time.

Megan's favorite thing about the lighthouse had always been the old, winding staircase that led up to the lamp room.

She stared wide-eyed up the steps, looking for the bloody footprints she'd seen the night before, but the stairs were bare. The old wood was worn from her and her father's boots, and the boots of the many lighthouse keepers before them.

But last night there had been footprints in blood.

I saw them!

Megan started a meticulous search of the lighthouse, checking every corner of every room and constantly afraid of what she'd find, but there was no sign that anyone besides herself had been there.

Her father had been drafted two years ago. They hadn't had a draft for decades; it was something everyone had thought belonged in the past, but the war in the Middle East was escalating, hitting closer to home each year. Her father was still young enough to fight, and Megan, at sixteen, had been deemed too old to be an excuse for him to stay, even as her only parent. She'd begged him to anyway, but he'd just smiled warmly at her, ever calm, and told her that fate is unavoidable.

He'd gone wearing confidence and pride. He'd gone willing and wanting to do his duty to his country. He'd gone, and left Megan.

She'd been the only occupant of the lighthouse for two years. Until last night.

Megan tried to tell herself it had just been a vivid nightmare but couldn't get the image of the footprints out of her head. In the hall outside her room, they had only been dark reflections on the floor, glistening softly in the little moonlight that shone in. Not knowing what they were at first, she'd followed them. She'd even gone up the first three steps before stopping under one of the tiny windows and crouching down to get a better look. The fright at discovering the truth of what they were had sent her fleeing back to her room.

They could not have been a dream.

Megan returned to her room and dressed in jeans and an old plaid shirt. Then she got out a pencil and paper and started to write a letter to her father.

Dear Dad, something strange happened to me last night. I got up from my bed to get a glass of water because I could not sleep, and I found a trail of bloody footprints in the hallway. I know this must seem absurd but...

She stopped. Her father was somewhere across the Atlantic, fighting for his life. His letters to her were already laced with worry. She couldn't add to his burden.

Megan put down her pencil and went to the kitchen to get the glass of water she'd been deprived of the night before. She sat on one of the stools while considering what she should to do. She had no other family to contact. Neighbors were miles away in each direction. With the footprints gone, the police would surely think she'd gone mad.

Maybe I should get a dog. A big dog.

Megan shook her head. She went to the stairs once more and went up as far as she had when she'd first found the prints, just to make certain they were, in fact, gone. She found nothing.

"Maybe it really was a dream." That's what she told herself for the remainder of the day while she did her chores and read a book and watched the sun set over the ocean from the lamp room—but the footprints were always lurking at the edge of her thoughts.

That night she crawled back into her bed and shut off the light. After three hours of begging for sleep to take her, she threw off the sheet and her heavy handmade quilt and opened her door.

Blood-red footprints glittered on the floorboards in the moonlight.

She slammed the door shut.

Megan ran to her nightstand and got her pocketknife. She looked at the admittedly pitiful weapon in her hands and decided that she could not spend another night wide awake, waiting for a possibly fictitious intruder.

She took her knife and left her room. The footsteps led to the stairs as they had before. She went up the first three steps then paused. The footprints disappeared from view around the bend of the wall. Her heart was beating so fast it hurt. She continued up, all the way to the top. The lamp room was dim, but the moon was brighter tonight. Bright enough for her to see the footprints leading all the way to the door to the balcony that rimmed the room. The door was closed, but when she opened it, the prints continued on the other side. They led right up onto the ledge of the balcony.

Megan's stomach lurched. She wasn't particularly afraid of heights, but the thought of someone standing there on the ledge, in the dark, made her skin prickle. You didn't survive a fall like that.

Megan closed the door and went back to her room, careful to avoid the footprints as she went down the stairs.

She hadn't realized she'd been holding her breath until she was back in her room. She resisted the urge to crawl up and huddle against the wall again, weeping. Instead, she got back in her bed and lay there till morning. She barely slept. When she did, she was tormented by nightmares.

She woke in a cold sweat, though she wasted no time leaving her room again and checking on the footprints.

An immediate, violent chill went through her upon opening the door. There was no sign of blood.

Megan dressed quickly and practically ran down to the main floor, grabbing the keys from the dish by the door and heading to the little blue pickup. Pebbles flew as she sped down the long dirt drive and turned right onto the main road. The nearest town was a twenty-minute drive.

Megan was trying to breathe normally. Her hands were vise-grips on the leather steering wheel.

The road was usually quiet, even more so this early in the morning. A light fog was still woven between the densely packed trees on either side of the road, and a ghostly layer hung half a foot above the asphalt.

Megan turned the radio on to distract her frantic thoughts. A cheery, upbeat song blared out of the speakers.

Megan thought of the footprints.

She turned the volume down to a whisper. Something about the carefree music was an eerie companion to her current mood.

What would she do once she reached the town? She hadn't thought out a plan before she left the lighthouse. She cursed her spontaneous flight. She'd let fear get the best of her.

"Okay, Megan. You have fifteen minutes to think of something rational." She took a deep breath. Tried to calm herself.

Who did you call about creepy, disappearing bloody footprints?

She'd already decided against the police—they'd think she was insane—but she needed someone to investigate. Would anyone believe her? Maybe someone who dealt with the supernatural. She wasn't sure she believed in ghosts, but after the past two nights and no rational explanation she could think of, she couldn't afford not to believe.

When she pulled into town, she went directly to the used bookstore. It wasn't just a bookstore; it doubled as a cafe and a general meeting place for every hipster, loner, and social outcast in town.

Megan parked, put a dollar in the meter, and went in. The bell above the door chimed, and a barista with a toque and ear spacers gave her a friendly smile. Megan tried to smile back but wasn't sure she'd pulled it off.

"Umm, can I have a small latte, please?" Megan said, resting her hands on the counter.

"Sure, that all?"

"Ah, yes, please."

"Sure thing. Three-fifty."

Megan dug for the change in her pocket and handed it to the girl. She walked, in what she hoped was a casual manner, to the corkboard by the door. It was filled with fliers and pamphlets and business cards. Someone was selling a lawn mower; another had kittens "free, but no shots". She searched the board for something she could use.

"One small latte."

There was a number for a vegan health coach. A fifty-percent-off coupon for knitting classes. Someone scalping tickets for a music festival.

"Miss? Your latte?"

There! A little purple business card for a professional medium.

Megan snatched the card and spun back around.

"Oh, sorry," she mumbled to the barista. She got her latte and walked one block to the ancient-looking pay phone. She didn't have a cell phone; service was impossible out at the lighthouse. Not to mention her father was somewhat of a technophobe. Megan had unfortunately adopted the irrational distrust of technology. It came from living off the grid for so long.

She dialed the number for the medium.

"Hello?" The woman on the other end had a deep, liquid voice.

"Um, hi. My name's Megan. Umm, I think—" *How can I possibly explain?* "—I think my house is haunted."

There was a short pause. "What makes you think it's haunted, darling?"

Megan swallowed. "Well, there are…apparitions."

"What kind of apparitions? Ghosts?"

Megan shook her head before remembering the medium couldn't see her. "No, no. Footprints."

"Footprints?"

Megan swallowed hard. "Bloody footprints."

There was another silence. Megan waited for more questions, but the medium seemed satisfied.

"I can certainly come check it out for you, see what I can find. Where do you live?"

She didn't really have an address. Just a mailbox number in town where her father sent his letters to. "Well, do you live in town? In Port Mayland, I mean."

"I do."

"Do you know the old lighthouse? The one off Peggy's Road?"

There was silence for a moment. "You live in an old lighthouse?"

"Yes. Yes, I do. When is the soonest you can come?"

"I have time tomorrow afternoon."

That meant another night alone, but Megan didn't have much choice. She could stay in a motel perhaps, but she didn't want to abandon the lighthouse. Even if there was a creepy ghost, it was home. "Alright, that's fine."

"See you then. Thank you for calling."

"Yeah, thanks."

Megan hung up and walked back to the truck.

The fog had burned off by then, but it had begun to rain. She passed a few cars on the way back, those who had to commute into town or beyond for work.

She was anxious about going back inside the lighthouse but couldn't stay outside in the rain. She went in and busied herself with more chores as the rain became thicker, heavy drops hitting the siding and echoing within. The clouds gathered and darkened, looking like dark tobacco smoke from a fisherman's pipe.

The rain clouds became a storm, and thunder tumbled overhead. Megan sat outside her bedroom door and waited with her flashlight and a large kitchen knife. At eleven thirty, the first footprint appeared. She'd imagined that they'd all appear at once. That she'd blink, and all of a sudden they'd be splattered across the floor. But instead, they came one at a time and slowly, step by step, made a ghostly procession up the stairs.

Megan rose shakily to her feet and followed.

She watched the footprints ascend and saw as they seemed to stop for a moment halfway up. A smudge of blood appeared on the wall beside them. Then they continued. Megan looked at the smudge as she passed and could almost make out what looked like a handprint. She shuddered.

She continued up after the prints as they made their way across the lamp room. She rushed to open the door before they got there and watched them step over the threshold and walk out onto the balcony. The wind howled, buffeting Megan with rain, but the persistent drops had no effect on the footprints. She could still see them as they stopped just before the ledge. Then, they appeared on the edge.

A brilliant bolt of lightning shot from the storm. It hit the lightning rod affixed to the roof of the lamp room with a crack so loud it seemed the earth had snapped in two. Megan screamed, covering her head with her arms, and tried to rush back inside.

She slipped on the rain-covered balcony and fell across the bloody footprints.

Her next scream died on her lips as the wind was knocked from her chest. She pushed herself up. Her clothes and hands were red. Her blond hair was streaked with blood. She scrambled inside, leaving the door open behind her. She ran down the stairs and back to her room and spent the rest of the night jumping at the sound of thunder and crying into her pillow.

The next morning, she woke up, damp and still exhausted. She went to the bathroom. There was no blood on her hands or clothes or hair as there had been the night before, but there was a small cut on her forehead. She must have gotten it when she'd fallen. The blood there had dried, and she had a hot shower to get herself clean.

After she was showered and dressed, the only thing on her mind was food. She hadn't realized how long it had been since she'd last eaten. The fridge was practically empty, and the medium said she wouldn't show until the afternoon, so Megan took the truck into town again.

She got breakfast at a twenty-four-hour fast-food place and ate it in the truck. Then she got a large coffee and took it with her as she walked to the post office.

"Morning, Meg," the clerk called.

Megan waved to the old woman. Her name was Susan.

"How are you?" she asked as Megan used her key to open her post office box.

"Oh, fine."

"You look tired, hun."

There was some mail. Mostly junk. A few bills.

And a letter from her father.

"Just nightmares."

Susan frowned. "Have you talked to anyone about them?"

Megan threw out the junk mail and walked over to the counter. "I'm seeing someone today, actually."

"Oh, I'm glad you're taking care of yourself, hun, what with your father away. Shame they wouldn't let him stay. You ever need anything, you just have to ask."

Megan smiled. "I know. Thank you. Could I get some stamps, please?"

The clerk brought out a small book of stamps and rang her in. Megan paid and returned to the truck. Usually, she would wait to get home before reading her father's letters, but she wasn't eager to return just yet. She threw the bills on the seat beside her and ripped open the brown envelope from her father.

Dear Megan, I hope you are doing well. The weather over here has been improving. Yesterday I met a man from the US. He's from California. He says it's quite nice there, and I think you would like it. Perhaps, when I am home again, we will visit. How would you like a road trip? Just the two of us? I'm afraid I don't have much time to write this, but I'll be home before you know it, sweetie. Love, Dad.

Megan wiped tears from her eyes. She could picture his thin, kind face. He had always worn a long white beard, but surely the military had made him shave it off by now. She missed him, so much so that just reading his words made her cry and feel intolerably lonely.

She drove back to the lighthouse. Just as she was getting out of the truck, a small black car was pulling down the drive.

"Sorry, I'm a little early," the medium said, stepping out of her car. She was a tall, black woman with neat, short hair and plain dark clothes. A large necklace of bright green, teal, and orange gems was the only pop of color she wore.

"That's alright," Megan said. She was relieved she could get this over with and didn't have to return to the lighthouse alone.

"My name's Rachel," the medium said, offering her hand to Megan.

"Megan. Nice to meet you."

Megan led her inside and showed her the main floor, then brought her up to the second floor, where the kitchen and bedrooms were. She explained how her father had bought and renovated the house and how he was away but would be returning sometime next year. They were standing at the bottom of the steps to the lamp room when Rachel finally spoke.

"So, besides this lighthouse being very old, what makes you think it is haunted?"

Here comes the part that makes me sound insane, Megan thought, taking a deep breath and then jumping into her explanation.

"Well, three nights ago I woke up in the middle of the night, and there were these bloody footprints in the hall. They led upstairs, to the lamp room, and they seemed to just end. On the ledge of the balcony."

"Bloody footprints?" Rachel's eyes were wide.

"Yes. And they've come back each night since. Last night, I stayed up and waited for them. It was like an invisible person was walking up the stairs, leaving the footprints behind."

Rachel still looked shocked. She turned to the stairs and pointed to them.

Megan nodded. "Yeah, they went that way."

She started up them, and Rachel followed.

When Rachel got to the top, she cautiously made her way to the balcony door and looked out. She stood there a while. She had her eyes closed and appeared to be either listening or thinking very hard. After a while, she shut the door again and turned back to Megan.

"There was a psychic who lived here before you? A long time ago?"

Megan felt her skin grow cold and resisted hugging herself. "I'm not sure."

"You have to tell me the truth," Rachel said, tone harsh. That irritated Megan. She didn't call her here to be accused of lying.

"That is the truth. But, well my father used to tell me stories about this place when I was a kid. Some of them had a psychic in them. She would read tarot cards up here while her husband worked the lamp," Megan said, gesturing toward the large bulb in the center of the room. "She'd make up all kinds of prophecies that always came true. But Dad made those stories up."

"He may have told you he made them up, but I doubt he did. Folklore like that often gets embellished, but there's always truth to it." Rachel walked past her and started down the stairs.

"Wait, where are you going?" Megan followed her.

"I can't help you. The spirit of the psychic is too strong. Likely she is still trying to tell prophecies."

"What?! You mean those bloody footprints are a prophecy of some kind?"

"It's likely. It's also possible her spirit is confused and is prophesying something that has already happened. My only advice is to look into the history and see if something took place here matching what you saw. If you find something, leave it out in the lamp room overnight. It could cure the spirit of its confusion."

Megan didn't know what to say.

Rachel looked at her, eyes sad, and then took something from her purse. It was a bushel of straw or some like type of plant.

Sage, Megan thought.

With a lighter from her pocket, Rachel lit it on fire and began wafting the smoke around the room.

Megan watched, silently, the smoke tickling her nose.

When Rachel had finished, she slipped the bushel into a plastic bag and put it back in her purse. She rested a hand on Megan's shoulder.

"That may cleanse the lighthouse of spirits, but some strong souls can hang on even after that."

With no further explanation of what "that" was, Rachel left.

And Megan was alone again with the lighthouse.

***

Megan sat on the floor of the lamp room, papers and old photographs spread out around her. The lighthouse keepers had left behind all sorts of stuff, and each new owner always kept it, adding their own things to the archive when they left. Her father had wanted to keep the tradition alive.

Megan picked up the photo of her and her father standing in the sand with their backs to the ocean. In the background of the photo, in the right corner, the lighthouse was just barely visible. She'd seen him put this photo, as well as a few other documents, into the archive before he'd left to fight. She'd never looked at them. It made it easier to pretend he hadn't done it.

She knew he'd wanted to add his own possessions, just in case he didn't come back from the war. Megan hated thinking about it.

She put aside her father's things and focused on the other, older items. Most were land deeds for the lighthouse and the surrounding property, browned photographs, and playing cards. There must have been twenty decks of playing cards. Megan guessed that's all there was to do when you were a solitary lighthouse keeper.

Megan sorted through the decks. Some had gotten wet at some point, their corners ripped or curled. Others had lost their packaging and were kept together with elastic bands. They were black, blue, or red. Some were more than one deck mixed together. Some were missing cards; others had too many. One deck was large print, so one of the lighthouse keepers must have had bad eyes—or maybe the big numbers simply made it easier to see in the dark.

There was one deck substantially larger than the others. Megan picked it up and removed the cards from their plain black box. Tarot cards.

Megan gasped and dropped them to the floor. They spilled out in a fan, revealing a photo that had been folded and tucked into the back of the box. Hesitantly, Megan unfolded it.

There was a young woman, with long dark hair pushed back from her face with a bandanna. She was sitting in the lamp room, in the very spot Megan was sitting. Tarot cards were spread out on the floor in a pattern that reminded Megan of a game of hopscotch.

The woman looked worried as she sat, examining the cards.

A breeze blew into the room, shuffling the papers. Megan had found nothing in the archive that would indicate that a murder or anything bad at all had taken place here. She sighed. She hadn't particularly wanted to discover a horrendous act had been carried out in the place she now called home, but it would answer questions. It would give some reason to what had been going on.

But it didn't matter. She had a new lead now.

She put everything but the tarot cards and the photograph back in the archive box, leaving her father's things on the top.

She took the photos and went out to the truck. The local library was far more extensive than it had any right to be for such a small town. But it was also a very old town, the kind that had a way of collecting history. Some of that history was on the strange side: ghost stories, records of lost ships, treasure buried on the nearby islands.

She found the section on the occult. She was expecting to find lots of old tomes with Gothic letters along the spines, but most of the books in the section were academic works. Lots of people studied the occult simply for its role in history, like alchemy and witch trials. These weren't helpful to Megan. She needed an instruction manual.

After reading the titles of fifty or more books, she came across one that sounded promising: *A Beginner's Guide to the Tarot.*

She slipped it off the shelf and flipped through the pages. There were diagrams and definitions and instructions for how to interpret multiple cards when placed together.

There were also diagrams in the back showing different patterns the cards could be arranged in. Megan found the one that looked like a hop-scotch board. The cards in the book were a newer style than the deck she'd found, with their simplistic, almost comic book figures, but the meanings were the same.

She closed the book and took it out at the desk. She felt embarrassed, taking out such an odd volume, but the librarian didn't give it a second glance, and soon Megan was on her way back to the lighthouse.

She spent the evening in her room, door closed, trying to figure out the tarot cards in the photograph. She laid them out just as they were in the picture and used the text as reference to understand what each card meant. Understanding the individual cards was easy, but putting their meanings together was more challenging. Some seemed almost contradictory to one another.

There was the High Priestess, the Tower, The Three of Swords, Death, and the Five, Seven, and Ace of Cups.

The High Priestess was at the bottom. Just above her was the Tower. That card frightened Megan. It was a tall gray tower being struck by lightning. The top of the tower was missing, knocked off by the lightning. She knew the time period would have made the tower a keep of some sort, but she couldn't help seeing it as a lighthouse. There were people falling from the tower, but it was impossible to tell if they'd fallen from the windows—or jumped from the top.

The Three of Swords was next, then Death. The Cup cards surrounded death. The Five on its right, the Seven at its left, and the Ace on top.

Megan noticed that in the picture, Death was upside down. She'd read in the text that sometimes, if you pulled a card from the deck and placed it upside down by mistake, it represented misunderstanding.

That wasn't very helpful. The one thing she needed most right now was to understand.

She looked at the notes she'd scribbled on a pad of paper.

The High Priestess could represent law or the divine will, but Megan figured she represented the psychic that used to live in the lighthouse.

Death represented, well, death.

The place the Three of Swords occupied was supposed to represent either the person reading the cards or the person whose fortune the reader was trying to see. The picture was a red heart run through by three swords. The background was rain and gray clouds.

What do I know? Megan asked herself, looking at her notes. *The High Priestess card is prophesying a disaster ending in death. The cups are related to relationships, communication, and mourning, and together they add to thirteen, an unlucky number. The three of swords is the person the prophecy is about, but there's nothing to indicate who that might be.*

Megan sighed and looked back at the photo. She noticed one more card in the psychic's hand. She could only barely make it out. The half she could see looked like swords. And there was a man too. She pulled the card close to read the Roman numerals at the top. VII. Seven of Swords.

Megan grew cold. She hurriedly flipped to page in the text that talked about that card. Her fears were confirmed. It was the thief card.

There's going to be a robbery. The cards could easily be prophesying my death!

Megan used one of the cards as a bookmark then put the rest of the cards and the photo back in the box and slipped them under the bed with the library book.

Just then, she noticed how dark it had gotten. She looked at the clock on her bedside. The footprints appeared just before midnight. She still had two hours.

Megan went downstairs and put on her boots, grabbed the keys, then marched out through the light rain to the shed. She opened the lock her father had put on the shed. It was the only one of the outbuildings on the property they kept locked. Inside, she groped for the string she knew was hanging to her left. She pulled it, and the lights came on.

At the back of the shed was a small gun cabinet. Being out in the cold and damp air wasn't good for guns, but her father never really used it and hadn't wanted it taking up space in the house. Megan prayed it still worked.

She opened the cabinet and removed the shotgun. Then, using yet another key, she opened the small drawer in the bottom to get at the ammunition. With shaky hands, she loaded the gun. Her father had shown her how some years ago, and she hadn't had a need to do it since.

Hoping she'd done it right, she locked up the cabinet and the shed and returned to her room.

She stood at the window with her loaded shotgun and watched the light rain turn into a thunderstorm that far outmatched the storm the night before. By eleven, it was shaking the building. It felt like it was hovering right above the lighthouse, putting down roots with its bolts of lightning instead of moving out over the ocean like it should.

Megan looked down at the driveway and saw lights moving toward the lighthouse. Her heart started to beat so furiously it was all she could hear, blocking out even the roaring thunder.

She put her back to the wall and tried to breathe. She held her gun ready. A shotgun wasn't meant for close quarters so she'd have to stay on the other side of the room from the door. That was fine with her. She wanted to be as far from the intruder as possible.

Minutes passed. She heard someone moving around in the kitchen. Then heavy booted footsteps in the hall. The intruder stopped right outside her door.

Tears were stinging Megan's eyes. She could barely see the door, but she heard the handle rattle. The intruder was trying to get in.

Megan whimpered, and she thought she heard the intruder say something, but the voice was silenced by the thunder and her racing heart.

There was the sound of a key in the door.

How did they get a key?!

Megan held up her gun.

The door swung open and a tall figure stood in the dark hallway outside her room. She only had a moment to think that he looked just like the mysterious figure on the Five of Cups before she shot. It took him in the chest, the buckshot not having enough time to spread out, making multiple dark spots on his green jacket.

Gasping for breath, Megan broke down the barrel. Her hands shook, and she cursed as she dropped the first shell onto the floor. She took another from her sweater pocket and pushed it into the chamber. She cocked the hammer and pulled the trigger for a second time. The shot went wide as she hadn't aimed, but it took the figure, now stumbling into her room, in the shoulder. He fell to the floor and didn't move.

Megan slid down the wall, crying. She broke down the barrel again. Another shell into the chamber. Cock. Aim.

A large pool of red blood was seeping out and spreading around the body. The intruder was wearing army camo.

I'll be home before you know it.

No. No, no, no!

"Dad!" Megan screamed and dropped the shotgun. She crawled to her father's body on hands and knees and rolled him onto his back. His eyes were open, staring up at nothing.

Megan clutched his jacket and collapsed onto his chest, weeping. "No. No, Dad. Come back. Please!"

She screamed until her voice was hoarse and her tears dried. She turned her head and, still lying on her father's chest, she saw the book and tarot cards lying under her bed. She crawled to them and took them out. She opened the book where she had stuck in a card to use as a bookmark. It was the Five of Cups, sitting upside down between the pages.

It symbolized loss, bereavement, and regret. It was the loss of a loved one.

Reversed, as it was now, it meant the opposite: a loved one coming home.

Megan took her pocketknife from the nightstand and stabbed the card and the book over and over again, only stopping when she'd hurt her hand too badly to continue.

A flash of lightning lit up her window, illuminating the silhouette of her father's body, quickly growing cold on the floor.

Megan picked up the book and the cards and stood. She collected the papers off her desk and then left the room, stepping over her father's body. The blood had spread too far to be avoided and it coated her feet in a slick layer.

She left the room and walked to the stairs. Halfway up the tears hit her again and she wavered, putting out a hand on the wall to catch herself. She left a print of blood behind. She didn't know if it was her father's or her own. Had she cut herself while stabbing the book? If so, she hadn't felt it. Even the ache of her likely sprained wrist had dulled now.

Megan continued up the stairs and went to the archive box. She removed the lid and put the things she carried into the box on top of her father's things. First went the book with the Five of Cups still between its now torn pages. Then the rest of the deck in its black box. Last went the letter her father had written to her, and on top of that, the letter she had begun to write to her father, never finished.

She put the lid back on the box and went to the door to the balcony. The wind whirled around the lighthouse, and lightning made the air hum. Megan looked behind her and saw the bloody trail of footsteps she'd left. Now she just had to finish them.

She put her hand in her pocket and removed another card. The Tower. The lightning. The people falling.

Falling? Or did they jump?

Megan knew the card wouldn't survive the waves. She dropped the card behind her; the sticky blood was the only thing that kept the wind from snatching it up.

The fate Megan had tried to avoid hadn't been hers in the first place. What if she'd read the signs right? What if she'd had more time? Would it have mattered?

Fate is unavoidable, she decided.

She stepped onto the ledge and looked down. Below, the waves of the Atlantic crashed against the rocks. You didn't survive a fall like that.

Beware the Autumn People

Melion Traverse

Early October wind licked down the street with the rollicking wisps of smoke-scent that sang of bonfires and the promise of jack-o'-lanterns. Jessa Mae drank in every flavor of that breeze, soaking it into her bones, spreading like the wildfire of youth through her muscles.

One-two, one-two.

Her legs pedaled faster as she hurtled with the wind sweeping at her back, carrying her with the crunch of fallen leaves that swooped with her tires. A rare thing, youth: when innocence and life twine themselves with the growing knowledge that responsibility and adulthood burn just beyond a girl's grasp. One ear listens to the high and wild songs of dragons and sword clashes, while the other strains for the barest hint at the jangle of car keys and every gulp of freedom.

The wind chewing at her hair and gnawing her face, Jessa Mae's world fell far away from the stretch of suburban sidewalks. Her bike was a horse—no, why stop there? why let everything press down upon the dreams?—it was a gryphon swooping across the skies with marrow-chilling clouds slipping past. Jessa Mae rode her gryphon all down the streets toward Granny's house and laughed into the autumn haze with the joy that children think no amount of years will ever wrest from their throats.

Born on the afternoon of March 19th, Jessa Mae was a Winter's child who passed for Spring. "It must have been important to you, being born in winter," her mother would remark with a smile warm as the last flash of the setting sun, "because you weren't waitin' for anythin'. Never have waited for anythin'. Wouldna wait but one more day—not my Winter's child."

But she never gave much thought to being a Winter's child because the colorful brush of spring burst too warm and glorious in her veins. Always moving, always asking, always fidgeting for something to do as though her skin couldn't quite contain everything that had to be done. She thought of herself, when it occurred to her to think on the matter at all, as a Spring's child born in winter simply because she was too curious to wait, too curious to miss a sun-burst moment of the spring which was hers both by right and by conquest.

Wheels spun clack-clackety-clack as Jessa Mae hurtled from her bike and raced up the rambling path, which led to Granny's porch.

She paused at a sudden frigid breath of wind that traced the back of her neck. Amid the October haze, a shade slicker than rain and darker than midnight's folds slipped out amid the autumn-bitten hydrangeas. The motion glided past the corner of her eye, and Jessa Mae whipped about, but only the breeze rustled the bushes, and she smiled at her own imagination. It was just daydreams bleeding into late afternoon shadows and wrapping themselves around thoughts of jack-o'-lanterns and chocolate.

The door was unlocked; it was always unlocked to Jessa Mae, who slap-slapped up the steps with scuffed sneakers.

"Granny! I'm here!" Jessa Mae called and entered the house that smelled of lilacs and creaked as though wind whispered through the walls. It was the sort of house that reached for Jessa Mae and wrapped around her in a hug of timber and stone, snuggling her to itself and letting her breathe just as she needed. She knew that the house drew its comfort from Granny, as though it stretched for her as an extension of the old lady, a body that could hold the young girl and let her cry, let her tremble, let her tell secrets that only old ladies remembering golden bursts of youth can fully understand.

Granny sat in a chair by the fireplace and sewed with threads gleaming as though spun from moonlight. Before her, the threads sparked and shivered as the elderly lady stitched them upon the thin air. Her fingers flicked through the air, and Jessa Mae realized that the old woman did not have a needle. Even more, the thread stretched from Granny's own fingers as though from a spool. Jessa Mae gazed with electric excitement in her blood: here was the magic that thrilled through her mind. And of course, it would be Granny who wove that magic; this Jessa Mae accepted as a reality as true as the skin over her bones.

Granny did not look from her work when Jessa Mae entered.

"And what were you today, my love?" The threads shimmer-sparked just a flicker more brightly. "Let me guess. Today you were a knight upon a unicorn riding for the sorcerer's tower."

"Close," Jessa Mae said, eyes tracing after the patterns in the air. "But it was a gryphon; last week was a unicorn. What's this?"

"A gift for you," replied Granny. "It is almost done—and not too soon, I fear. While I finish, fetch yourself a mug of tea, and then come right back because we must talk about serious things."

Jessa Mae hesitated, feet firm on the floorboards but thoughts spiraling to the rafters. Time to time, she and Granny talked about "serious things," but always when Jessa Mae started on the topics. Mean girls at school who wrote nasty things on her desk or stupid boys who pulled her hair and called her names. Those were the serious things Jessa Mae carried to Granny and laid before the elderly lady with expectations of answers.

At a nod from Granny, Jessa Mae broke from her mental wanderings and fetched a cup of tea.

The girl returned with a mug that steamed its sharp spice into her face, filled her nostrils, and soaked into the autumn chill beneath her ribs.

"You are a Spring's child," said Granny as she worked the silver thread.

"Mom says I'm a Winter's child—born one day before spring," answered the girl, and she burned to ask about the magic, but she understood Granny knew the questions trembling on Jessa Mae's tongue. Granny would answer when she got to answering.

"She's wrong. Spring lights all through you, sinew and heartbeat alike." Weave, stitch, weave. "I'm a Summer's child, born in the humidity of the last stretch of August, lived my life as though everything was burning, and I had to race it all. But you, you race to get in front of everything, dart about seeking where it will all go, how it will all unfold like flowers pressing from the soil.

"Your brother," Granny continued, "he is an Autumn's child, striking a course on that edge between too hot and too cold, old before his time."

Jessa Mae nodded, sort of understood in the way that she understood most deep truths: not in her mind, but somewhere past her lungs and down to her fingertips. She thought of little Tommy who toddled about the world with deliberate purpose guiding his steps, peering out at a world to be turned and examined, pressed in his hands and held aloft to ponder from each angle and then set aside as he laced together the meaning of everything. Jessa Mae saw it in how he played with his toys, figuring each bit from the other and ordering it with the precision of an emperor wise in a world that has since fled through time. She was dash and hurry; he was contemplation and wonder.

"I 'spose he is," Jessa Mae admitted. "But what's this all about?"

"He's an Autumn's child," Granny repeated. "They will come to try and claim him, the Autumn people will."

An ice-rain chill dribbled along Jessa Mae's spine. She had never heard of the Autumn people, but Granny's voice hardened from lilac petals to oak wood at the name.

"You do not know who they are," Granny continued as she watched the girl's expression. "No, of course not. They touch upon the shadow-tips of the late-born Summer's children, but they have no dealings with Spring's children. But Autumn's children? Autumn's children they claim as their own, they drift toward them and claw for them, seek out their worlds and their dreams and drink them into themselves.

"Beware the Autumn people, my child. They are those who lost youth and all of its dreams because they drifted too far from summer and borrowed from a winter not their own, and it pulled them from their bones one strand at a time, unraveled them even as they lived. Now they are shades that must gulp at the dreams of others and will call them into the shadows to haunt eternity at their sides. Misery is their meat, and pain is their drink."

Jessa Mae remembered the slip of shadow darker than midnight's folds vanishing into the hydrangeas. The thought went cold to her guts. But hadn't that been the echoes of daydreams and nothing more?

"T-tommy?" she chattered his name through teeth rimed with frost from the freeze deep in her stomach.

"Yes, Tommy. But you can save him, Jessa Mae. You *must* save him." Granny rose from her chair, held forth something that Jessa Mae could see only by the dimming flits of shimmers. "I started sewing this two days ago, and I have done nothing else. It is summer blended with spring and the

Autumn people will fear it; they will recoil before it like wolves at a fire."

Jessa Mae set aside the mug. "What is it? Why should they fear it?"

"It is a cloak."

A cloak? "You mean, like Little Red Riding Hood?" Jessa Mae scoffed before she caught herself and ducked her head guiltily.

"No, my child. She was foolish, and you are not. This is not a cloak for a silly little girl, but for a warrior facing battle." Granny motioned Jessa Mae closer. "It is time for the world you live to borrow from the world you dream."

Granny settled the cloak across Jessa Mae's shoulders—*It has weight*, she thought, surprised to feel the heaviness of fabric hanging from her shoulders—and Granny fastened a clasp at Jessa Mae's throat.

"I have sewn this with the thread of life itself," Granny said. "It is a patchwork of all my happy memories, many of which involve you, my child. Every shining moment, every bright dream I ever nourished, every smile that I can pull from my mind, those are all stitched together into a fabric that the Autumn people dare not touch. I am summer, and you are spring; together we will save your brother."

"What should I do?" Jessa Mae asked, stroking the cloak that hung over her shoulders; lines like shooting stars flickered under her touch.

"Go to your brother, wrap him in this cloak, and command the Autumn people away. Command them that he is *your* brother, that you will watch over him, that they will never have him. Then keep this cloak close to you, dear as your own skin. Understand?"

Jessa Mae nodded because words seemed too small.

"Go now, my child. Go with my love, my dreams, and my memories." Granny's arms went around Jessa Mae's shoulders with less weight than even the cloak.

"I *will* save Tommy," Jessa Mae promised. "I will, and then tomorrow, I will come back to carve a jack-o'-lantern for you." Granny smiled, and it was the warmth of candlelight in gourds, memories of every year when Jessa Mae left a single lop-sided grinning jack-o'-lantern on the porch to ward away mischief-makers who came prowling about old homes in darkness.

"Go ride your gryphon and save your brother," Granny ordered, and Jessa Mae obeyed.

Cloak fluttering down her back, Jessa Mae ran from the house and righted her bike. Granny, wise in many things, had cut the fabric short enough that the girl could still ride her bike without the dreams and memories entangling in the wheels. Jessa Mae put all of her muscle into her pedaling, did not look back at the house, clack-clackety-clack down the walkway, jumped her bike over the curb, and sped like the breath of Zeus down the street.

Deep afternoon was sinking into the grasp of twilight, and the shadows lunged from trees, grasped at Jessa Mae as she pedaled harder, faster, harder again down the street. Shadow moved among the shadows; the rain-slick shades had found her and leapt alongside the girl as she raced them home. On both sides, the movement gathered speed. Blinks of orange—bright and hot as jack-o-lantern smiles—sparked within the shadows. Harder Jessa Mae pedaled, pumping her legs and leaning over the handlebars, each thump of her heart a desperate jolt of power pushing her onward. The Autumn people pulled beside her, a slithering and speeding mass of lightless hunger. Then they surged ahead.

"You can't have my brother!" Jessa Mae hollered into the deep October wind.

Another path—gravel-strewn and treacherous—spun off from the road. It would be quicker; she rarely followed it for fear of the sharp turns, the jutting tree branches. But the shadows flowed up ahead, pulling away even as she pedaled for all the speed her muscles could summon.

The Autumn people could not win. Sweat sharp in her eyes, slick on her hands, Jessa Mae thought of the cloak, of Granny and the old lady's faith that Spring's child could prevail. Today the girl must be brave. A deep breath, and she hopped her bike over the curb and swept down the fearful path. Gravel sprayed from her tires; the bike slipped, slid, wobbled. Jessa Mae's breath caught hot in her lungs as she fought first one way and then the next, desperate to keep speed and not go sprawling off the bike. She called upon the dreams of riding gryphons, of holding their reins in her hands as the great beasts swooped and dove. She did not panic then; she could not afford to panic now. Fingers away from the brake levers, she drew the calm of dreams deep into her nerves.

She pulled from the skid, righted the bike. Adrenaline pulsing, Jessa Mae laughed in triumph and relief. Leaning once more over the handlebars, she pedaled for all she could. A branch tore her sleeve, gashed her arm. The cloak fluttered behind her in sparks of an old woman's dreams. The autumn leaf smoke blurred with the traces of lilac left from Granny's fingers, and Jessa Mae drank it all to the depths of her lungs, pushed it through her muscles, and flung it back out in the burst of speed that carried her home.

She sped off the path in a clattering rattle as she jumped her bike from the curb. Her street—her street on which nestled a house unaware of the terror spilling toward it—stretched like an asphalt ribbon. She chanced a look back over her shoulder. An orange blink in moving shadows. The Autumn people. The shadows roiled now like angry water, grasping as they flooded down the street.

Jessa Mae hurled aside her bike with the wheels all clattering as they spun. In panting breaths, she threw open the front door and saw a single shade—faster than the others, probably hungrier and more dangerous, too—glide in at her heels. *Tommy!* Her mother shouted something about doors and barns, but Spring's child was dashing forward, always moving, always looking.

Tommy stood in his crib with contemplative eyes that peered through ages fixed not on Jessa Mae but on the shade that bit at her sneakers. He raised a confused whimper and reached for his sister, chubby arms grasping to be pulled away from the hungry shadows spilling through the door.

Jessa Mae snatched hold of him. He clung to her neck, face hot against her shoulder as he trembled. A half-dozen phantasmal arms grasped for the future of one little boy. Jessa Mae saw the stretch of shadow and whirled away, pressing herself between the boy and the shade. If they wanted Tommy, first, they would have to reach past her.

The howl of pain went electric-white in Jessa Mae and she breathed for a moment as though the pain was hers. But it was the shade and its agony because it had grasped for the boy and clutched instead the cloak that shot sparks like stars bursting far in the night.

For an instant, Spring, Summer, and Autumn intermingled amid the guttering silver shine. Jessa Mae cocooned her brother deep inside the cloak, hugging him tight, as though she could wrap her whole body around him and hide the toddler from the grasp of the Autumn people.

One shade let go, but another slid along the wall, another across the floor, a third over the ceiling. More choked the doorway. Deep puddles of thirst and greed, hungering for the even deeper dreams of the little boy. The autumn chill leached into Jessa Mae's bones, crawled her flesh, worked her own dreams into nightmares.

"Granny," Jessa Mae whispered into the curly tufts of her brother's hair. He whimpered in response, trailed into the beginnings of a yowl, sensing even more keenly than his sister what reached toward him.

"Autumn people!" Jessa Mae shouted. "You can't have my brother! I am Spring's child, and I have summer in my cloak! I will never let you take him! He's mine! He's his own! He can never be yours!"

The most shining moments in a woman's long-lived life pulsed against the shadows. Screams that echoed not in ears, but in bones and in teeth, that battered into skulls and wormed into brains.

Jessa Mae held her brother closer still, wrapped the cloak tighter—it *must* cover him; she could face the attack like the knights with gryphons and swords. The screams grew, pressed against her skull, threatened to explode her apart.

"Go away!" Jessa Mae ordered in the voice of clashing swords, and the cloak responded with another burst of radiant stitching.

A final shriek brought Jessa Mae to her knees, and then the silence filled her like a wash of cool rain against fevered skin. It was over. The Autumn people had gone. For a moment longer, she held fast to her brother and stroked his head with fingers that trembled as much as the boy she tried to console.

"Ssh," she whispered. "They're all gone now. You're safe, I promise."

One more hug and then she set him back into his crib. She handed him his stuffed animal.

Jessa Mae folded away the cloak in the nightstand by her bed. Close at hand, always, just as Granny had ordered. *Thank you, Granny. Thank you for your dreams and for the brightest moments. I love you.*

***

The wheels of her bike spun a lazy clack-clackety-clack where it lay on the lawn as Jessa Mae bounded up the porch steps. Out in the garden, tumbled together in an orange-burst tangle, were Granny's pumpkins, and Jessa Mae would choose the biggest, the best, and carve it with the widest smile she had ever carved. The jack-o'-lantern would grin and laugh in fluttering light against all of the mischief-makers, both of flesh and of shadow.

But although the house creaked its welcome as before, and although the scent of lilacs teased the air, Jessa Mae did not find Granny seated in her chair by the fireplace. Nor in the kitchen, nor out in the garden.

Jessa Mae knew. She knew it all to her soul and up through her bones. Granny was gone, had been gone long before, her body carried away and buried like the pumpkin seeds. Dreams and memories remained. Dreams and memories that she had sewn from her fingers into a patchwork cloak, joining spring and summer for always.

She left Granny's house that night for the last time, her hands scented with pumpkin flesh, as she returned home to the cloak and a life of watching for the Autumn people. On the porch, against mischief-makers who would sneak about an abandoned house, a large jack-o'-lantern flickered light from a wide, triumphant grin. Granny would have smiled just as brightly.

The Renewal

Hanna Day

Shivers crawled down Loretta's spine as she emptied the ceramic basin over her head. She blinked away water, a stinging pain erupting on the backs of her hands as the water dripped over the exposed gouged flesh. Gooseflesh rose on her bare skin as a cool breeze fluttered in through her window, bringing with it the faint smell of autumn.

She didn't look at the slab of mirror hanging on her wall as she squeezed water from her long brown hair into the bucket on the floor. A white cassock hung on the door, plain and unadorned, waiting as she prepared for the Renewal.

Loretta wished she had kept quiet all those months ago. If she had not spoken up, shared her dreams and asked for their meaning, she would not be here now. No matter how many times she bathed, she couldn't wash away a creeping, oily feeling that had settled upon her earlier that morning, like a thin layer of grease lingering on one's hands after washing a cooking pan, repelling soap and water.

She scrubbed herself dry, taking care to go behind the ears and in between the creases of her fingers, the rough towel sloughing away the scabs softened by the water. Her damp hair fell across her forehead and shoulders. Droplets of water trickled down her neck as she pulled her hair into a bun. It would not do to have her hair in the way for the ritual.

A tightness knotted her shoulders as she pulled the cassock over her head, a tightness that had lingered for months. Blood smeared the sleeve as she pulled a hand through it. She paused. It would only take a moment to heal the small wound. No matter. Her clothing would be discarded after tonight anyway. She stepped backward, something moist soaking the hem of her cassock and the space between her toes.

Water soaked the floor. A shadowy patch spread slowly across the brown prayer mat, darkening as she stepped on it to assess the damage. She tilted her head. Better take care of it. Water would damage the simple embroidery stitched by her own hands just after her ordination. A symbol of her dedication, her faith, the colors worn from kneeling upon it five times a day.

Extracting the water would waste time. Time she did not have. Time no one had. But the ritual happened every one hundred years—surely, it could wait a little longer.

Thump.

Loretta froze as she felt a vibration underneath her feet. Her colleagues, who had not wasted time like she had, were already congregated in the belly of the monastery. Warning her. Calling her. *You're wasting time*, it seemed to say. *You promised to perform the Renewal.*

Loretta clasped her hands over her face, her fingers cupping her nose and mouth, her breath unnaturally loud in the palms of her hands. She didn't want to go, didn't want to face them, didn't want to keep her promise. For speaking of the ritual, organizing it, setting the preliminary Songs ahead of time—seemed distant from the actual deed. She had never done this before, and something would go wrong.

But her colleagues compelled her. Bound her to them a year ago, their collective will overcoming her protestations in a moment of weakness.

Because you're selfish.

She shut her eyes, once again feeling the pulse beneath her toes. *Be grateful.* Being able to feel a pulse at all was a precious gift. Her fingers left a film upon her cheeks, and she wished to wash again, or else the sweat and grease would sting her eyes. Taking a deep breath, she ignored this impulse, pulled on her soft shoes, and left her room.

"You're late, Mater." A black-clad guard straightened as she walked out.

She could not trust herself to say anything at all. Her hands folded together, fingernails dragging over tender skin.

He eyed her hands. "You should take care of that."

At this, she tucked her hands inside the sleeves of her robes, forming fists as her fingernails dug into the flesh of her palms.

"I will, Captain," she replied, looking at a point beyond his shoulder. "Let us proceed."

"Of course, Mater."

They walked past the nave toward the back of the sanctuary. The doors were already closed for the day. Despite this, she saw more black-clad figures patrolling amongst the pews. No one could be allowed in today. Not for anything.

She knelt in front of the altar and looked up at the great stained-glass window above her. Sunlight filtered through, casting her in hues of blue and red. A young woman and two men knelt on a snowy mountaintop, their hands reaching for the stars, exalted faces turned toward the Composer above. Thanking the Composer for the gift. A gift with too high a price.

The artist had managed to give the blood running down their necks a vibrant hue. Their cheeks flushed with color, and their clothes were free of bodily fluids. As a child, she thought the glasswork beautiful, the glowing glass numinous in its vastness. But now, whenever she looked at it, all she could see was the deep blood-red. Its light spread over her, as though to remind her just how deeply she was wrapped in its charnel embrace. The gruesome process of death beautified by an artist's hand, for how else could the priests confront it?

Loretta bent her head and gave thanks. They had sacrificed so much, and it would be a dishonor to stop the ritual after all these years. And yet, she wished she hadn't uttered her gratitude. The words lingered like a tasteless, rubbery lump of fat too large to chew but too improper to spit out as a shapeless, slimy wad in front of guests.

***

An unnatural stillness permeated the air as Loretta descended the spiral steps, steadying herself against the cold stone walls with a trembling hand. Her colleagues had prepared the sacrifices beforehand, and though she had seen them before in her vision, this would be their first and final meeting.

The pulse grew with every step and now thundered through her bones. The tightness between her shoulder blades spread to the rest of her body. Her lungs shriveled in the increasing chill, refusing to work properly as she struggled to breathe. A shooting pain locked her legs, and a rush of air leapt into her throat as she missed a step, her feet tripping over her cassock as she tried to find her footing.

A hand snatched her arm, fingers digging painfully into her flesh as they pulled her back to her feet. A shadow fell over her, the guard's head blocking out the torchlight. One of the guards waited for her to continue, his expression impassive.

"Careful, Mater."

She glanced down, studying the hand still clenched around her arm. In any other time, she would have reprimanded him for daring to touch her, his grip lingering longer than necessary, but she deserved it. She deserved this pain. Welcomed it.

Their eyes met. She saw nothing but coldness, and she envied it. He was more obedient to the faith than she was. As he let go, she could almost feel the blood pooling beneath her skin, forming dark bruises that would not disappear for weeks. A tremor passed through her, a brief, dangerous thought suffusing her mind: she could run. Run right into him, run back up the stairs into the safety of the sun, and forget the darkness beneath them. But what would be the point then? It would only confirm what so many suspected: that she was unfaithful.

A heretic.

She trembled at the thought. That was what she was: a weak link amongst her peers, requiring damage control, and punished for her conscience by being selected to perform the Renewal. Disagreement could not be tolerated. No variation of the ritual allowed because they had all been tried before. And afterward, what was to stop them from killing her? Or being driven insane by the others by the very system she helped maintain or slaughtered by the guard accompanying her now?

No, they couldn't. The world knew her. The queen considered her a friend, unsuspecting of her depravity. Her students would wonder why she had gone. Her aging parents would mourn. She would be left alive in a hell of her own making.

The moment passed, and she walked on.

Her apprehension washed away as she approached the Renewal chamber, the pulses so great there seemed to be no pause between them, and her every step in time with the constant rhythm. The stone hallway opened to a large room, cavernous and immense in her growing uneasiness. Fresh candles lit her way, illuminating the brilliant white cassocks her fellow councilmembers wore. Just like hers, they were devoid of all decoration denoting rank.

The other seven knelt in a circle surrounding a great stone slab, their faces turned to the floor. None of them looked up as she entered the room. A rush of cold air flushed between her legs as the wind found its way through the cracks in the walls.

Five guards stood at multiple points of the circle, their black uniforms blending into the darkness, stony sentries who would do nothing. Unless something went wrong. Loretta wondered if there was anything she could do—anything at all. Music—for what other word could be used to describe the magic of this world—pumped through her blood, infusing her, allowing her to sense the emotions of others in the room down below. Their apprehension spiked.

"Mater," the guard said. "Your hands."

She looked down at her hands, the skin dry and raw. Blood underneath her fingernails from all the times she scratched, and scratched, and scratched. Loretta flexed her hands, feeling the sting as her healing skin stretched with her joints. There would be scarring once they healed. If they ever did at all.

The hairs on the back of her neck rose as the guard took her hands, a deep, low hum rumbling through him as he began the healing Song. An itch, so powerful it seemed to seep into her bones, erupted on her skin as the wounds began to heal. Loretta wrenched her arms away, tucking them underneath her armpits.

"Mater…" He spoke as though to a small child. Like a mother wanting her child to sit still so she could heal a scraped knee with a lullaby.

"Leave it, Captain." The cardinal, an older man who had been in his position since Loretta was a child, did not look up as he spoke. "Join us, Loretta. *Now.*"

Loretta took her place in the missing space, though she did not kneel like the others. She stood there, her eyes fixated on the stone slab, upon which three still figures lay.

The smallest body caught her eye first. A child. Dressed in identical funeral clothing, from a distance the sacrifices were white, genderless, faceless with funeral shrouds—with one hand placed over their hearts—they seemed *above*. Beyond. Separate from the rest of humanity. As she took a step closer, the cloth moved slightly, caving in and billowing out with their hot breath.

"They're still alive." The words tumbled out of her before she could stop herself. Loretta wasn't certain what she expected—she already knew this. But saying it out loud, confirming it with the others—it would give her time.

"The ritual cannot proceed if they are dead." Eric, the kneeling figure to her right, looked up at her.

Dead, dead, what was dead to her? To them? To the people of this country? But these sacrifices were Silent— born without magic. Even if they were unconscious, she should be able to feel their emotions. At least sense that they were alive. So strange to her that these people were alive, but she could not sense their heartbeats.

"It will be merciful, what we're doing," Eric said.

She understood, yes, understood but did not accept. At least, a small part of her did not. But these people on the slab, on an altar hidden away in the deep, dark confines of the monastery, hid a secret from the entire world by their mere existence. For no one, no one except those present, knew that the original sacrifice to bring magic into the world wasn't the end.

"Our magic," Eric whispered, "it will be gone if you do not do this."

One of her fellow councilwomen broke away from the circle and knelt before her, opening a wooden box for Loretta's inspection. A knife lay upon soft gray silk, its blade gleaming in the dim light.

The knife was a beautiful thing—the blade made of black stone, grooved so blood could flow smoothly through. When Loretta picked it up, the worn leather felt comfortable, as though it had been made for her.

The knife wavered in her grip. How could she know this would work? Could she be certain? Could she have ever known that she would be here, a woman of the church, preparing for a ritual to renew the world magic?

She had been born with the Music, as everyone else had, learned how to use it to connect with one another. After she took up the cloth, the Council revealed the renewing ritual to her. Convinced her of its importance. The ultimate gift from the Silent, who could contribute nothing else to this lowly sphere.

Loretta reached out to touch the shroud—she deserved to see the child's face. Despite all the preparation, all the prayers, all the visions, she couldn't prepare herself for this.

"Please, let me see them."

"Don't," Eric said, grasping her hand. "It will make it harder for you."

She wrenched her hand away and pulled the shrouds from the bodies.

The girl was no older than eight. Two others lay beside her—a middle-aged man, his face darkened and swollen from a contusion, and a frail old man, his skin loose, a man near the end of his natural life. Or so she assumed. What she would like to believe.

Loretta's eyes lingered on the child. What did her parents think? Many who had Silent children gave them up, but there were a few who did not. Some drowned their children in the River Eoi. Left them in the woods. Smothered them in their sleep. It was easy to judge them, those murdering parents, but did they know the truth? Did they kill their babes so the priests would not?

Perhaps, if she had a Silent babe who could survive until the next Cycle, when the ritual would be performed again, then she would too.

She shivered at the thought.

The girl's face was pale, already the pallor of death. A hue the colored glass in the sanctuary could not capture. She looked so much like Loretta's niece—an ebullient girl with a knack for mathematics. Wanted to follow in her aunt's footsteps as a priestess. A path she should never have to take. Not when it could lead to this.

"We can't do this," Loretta whispered.

"None of us wanted this!" a councilmember snapped. "This is the only way to renew our magic. Sing the binding Song now."

She had come this far. Any rescue attempt for the sacrifices would fail, and another priest would take her place.

It must be done.

Loretta took a deep breath and released it with a Song. It began as a gentle hum as she sought out the starting note, unsure if she could perform it correctly with her emotions so tangled, then gradually rose into a crescendo. The others joined in, and together, they formed a powerful chord. She led the melody as a conductor leads an orchestra, her hands wavering as she kept the time. All eight councilmembers—including herself—became *connected*. Exposed, her emotions stripped naked from her corporeal body as they fused with the others, becoming one. As the song ended, a deep, deep pulse echoed in the cavern. A great thumping noise, precisely timed. And as she looked up at the ceiling, she felt as if she occupied the heart of a gigantic creature so immense its heart beat once every one hundred years, and she was here to keep its heart pumping full of blood so that the other organs may survive.

The councilmembers looked at one another, compelled to do so by her actions, by the magic now tethering them. Connected as they were, they could not help but follow her. Feel each other's apprehension. Understand the emotional state of each and every person performing the Renewal. The cardinal, indistinguishable from his subordinates, fought against the magic as he stood up. His gray eyes bored into hers. Accusing. Loretta could not look away. Whatever he had to say, she deserved it after all of the trouble she'd caused.

"They cannot be killed all at once," the cardinal said. "Else it will not renew correctly."

"I know." She did not bother with the honorific attached to his position. Why should he feel the need to tell her the obvious? Why now?

Judging from his Tune, the cardinal felt the slightest apprehension. No one had performed the ritual in a hundred years—how could they be certain? What if they were wrong, and there was another way?

But there they were: the three people she had seen in her vision. A child taken from her parents. A criminal who would not be missed. An old man at the end of his life. Not every Silent person could become a sacrifice. Not everyone could see the symptoms, have the patience to hunt them down, to try to understand what was happening. It was only fitting that she finished what she had started.

But a child? Why a child? What god would do this?

The middle-aged man—*Thomas, his name is Thomas*—shifted, his hand sliding back to his waist. A fellow councilmember reached over her, gently pulling the funeral shrouds back over the bodies. Bodies. As if they were already dead.

They were bound by something she could not quite describe—as though it were something bigger. A powerful magic more heavy and ancient, something greater than she. It permeated the room, suffusing, her anxiety reaching out toward the others. Changing them. Influencing all except the three still figures. Strange, how the unearthly Music only selected people unable to perform magic for its Renewal. A divine punishment, some of her colleagues said, for an impure soul.

She looked back toward the sacrifices. *Selfish.* The word rebounded in her mind, tumbling in circles like the

Cycle of magic coming to an end. How could this be, with what she understood of the world?

"The Cycle is ending," councilwoman Alynna said, an irritated edge to her voice. "Loretta, you must act now."

Loretta could sense the magic waning. The world wavered; her senses dimmed. It had been dimming for some time. She had never lived without the magic, didn't know life without it, so it had to be done—

Selfish.

"The people have to know." She looked up, causing the others to do so as well. "After it's done, tell the people—"

"We've gone through this before!" Alynna stood up, with difficulty, as they were still bound together. "This is the only way it can be done! If it were unregulated, if people understood…more of *them* will die." She pointed to the sacrifices. "There will be chaos."

Their armies depended upon it. Without the Music, society would fall. Generals unable to bind their soldiers together with a Song. Husbands and wives unable to understand what the other was thinking. People wouldn't be able to connect with one another, understand one another—

Selfish.

Selfish for wanting the ritual to move forward, to renew the Music despite its high price. Selfish for wishing for someone else to complete the task. They could allow the sacrifices to awaken, try to make them understand, convince them to perform the ritual themselves, but they couldn't risk losing the magic. Couldn't risk waiting another hundred years until the next Cycle. Loretta imagined kneeling next to the girl, showing her how to slit her own throat, placing the knife in her too-small hands.

No. It was better this way. She was their leader. She alone knew the sacrifices' names. Even in death, they would be remembered. She would be sure of it.

The council circled around the stone. Bile roiled at the back of Loretta's throat as she gripped the knife. She had never killed anyone before. What made everyone believe that she could do it now, when it mattered the most? Loretta moved to the head of the stone slab and reached out to touch the child's neck. Although the child was imbued with magic, through a process Loretta did not understand, she still could not feel the child's heartbeat. Perhaps, then, she should not feel sorry for them. How could they truly be alive when you couldn't even sense a heartbeat?

Selfish.

No one asked to be born with magic. No one asked for this to happen. But to have the prerogative to take away what belonged to the masses—

Selfish.

Take away a child from her parents. For the child to die without understanding her sacrifice, her contribution to the world, was a sin. But a necessary sin.

Nothing but a selfish—

She closed her eyes as she tilted the child's head back and pressed the knife to her neck. A soft moan distracted her. Blood spotted the shroud, spreading as the child stirred.

Loretta collapsed to her knees, tears bursting from her as the knife fell from her hand and clattered onto the floor.

"What if I'm wrong?" she exclaimed. "It can't be a child!"

"It doesn't matter now!" Eric snapped. He stood up, breaking the circle. "We're almost out of time!"

She turned to him, scooping up the knife as she did so. Gasps filled the room as the other priests rose, some grabbing at Eric as the others stepped away, allowing the guards to come into the circle. The man who had escorted her caught her wrist. She trembled.

"Our blood won't work," Eric said, breathing heavily. "Volunteers have already been tried. You know that."

"Maybe we haven't found the right ones," Loretta whispered.

"Even if we can, there's no time. If you don't do this now, we'll have to wait another hundred years for the Renewal."

"But—"

"Fates, woman!" Eric exploded. "We've had years to argue! We made our decision!"

Someone grabbed her wrist. Loretta looked up and realized that one of the guards had taken hold of her. Blood dripped down the back of her hand—the one holding the knife. The other quivered, wanting to continue her incessant scratching. She wanted to scratch. Wanted to feel something—anything—to punish herself.

She gazed at her fingertips, wondering if they had ever been clean, had ever been free of her own flesh since preparing for the Renewal. Loretta took a shuddering breath and nodded. The guard let her go, and she moved back toward the center of the circle.

Loretta had never killed anyone before. The science of it baffled her. Preparation for the Renewal included learning the quickest way to kill someone. A blade to the neck. Slice it there, and they will bleed out within minutes. It chilled her so, imagining how easy it was to kill someone.

"Just do it," Eric whispered.

Her body seemed to move on its own. Loretta felt as if she were looking upon herself, her mind protesting but her body following the pulse of Music. The knife slid through flesh easily, sliding over the bones and tissue without thought for the soul within. Thick, hot blood splashed across her face, forcing its way between her lips and coating the roof of her mouth. She spluttered, spitting out the foul, metallic taste already sliding down her throat.

Fighting the urge to retch, Loretta moved to the men, her eyes focused on the stone wall opposite her, flinching as the old man jerked in death. At the end of one's life, one heard a strange Music floating through the air—a memory, the essence of their being dying in a brilliant display of magic—but Loretta heard nothing. Had she done it wrong?

The silence permeating the room suddenly deafened. A great wind swept through the room, causing the candles to flicker into darkness and blowing the funeral shrouds away. Sticky strands of hair clung to her cheeks as she looked up, wiping away the spittle dribbling down her chin. A warm wetness soaked the sleeve of her cassock, though she didn't want to look, didn't want to see how drenched she was.

Thin tendrils of light snaked from the sacrifices' mouths, twirling around each other, as though they were searching for one another. Loretta reached out and grabbed them. They trembled feebly. If she did not do this, then they would transform into Celestial Spirits—ghosts of their former selves. Blood dripped from the knife as she reached up and sliced through them, severing them completely from this world.

Faith in the Composer—faith in the ancient magic—filled her. Faith that this ritual would renew the magic overcame her. Loretta's gaze fell to the bloodied knife in her hand. Relief spread through the council, suffusing her, calming her in her moment of panic.

"It is done," she whispered.

Loretta stood still. The pulse slowed, and her bones no longer shook. She lifted her shaking hands to her face, her fingers curled as she suppressed a scream. She was too selfish to turn the knife upon the council who performed this ritual of Renewal once every hundred years. Too selfish to stop this from happening.

Better them than me.

Selfish.

It only happens every hundred years.

Selfish.

Sacrifice others for the greater good.

"Loretta." It was Eric's voice. "You can put the knife away now."

The sacrifices had names. They had families and loved ones who would never see them again. They were also no one, people selected and chosen from the streets. No one would mourn them or even know how they died.

"Loretta." His voice again, more urgent.

A scream erupted from her. Men caught her arms, wrestled the knife away as she struggled against them. She barely felt the pain as she began scratching her hands, more forcefully and intensely than before. Her hands tore at her clothes, at her sticky hair, at the metallic taste still lingering on her tongue.

Smoke stung her eyes as her colleagues lit the funeral pyre, and for a moment, she wondered if she could bring down the rocky cavern down upon them all with her Renewed magic. Suffocate them all in rock and smoke, for what else were they now that the Renewal was complete? Even if her life was not enough to restore the ancient magic, her death could, at least, make noise when nothing else could.

Curse the Composer!

But why? He had done nothing except show her the way to Renewal. She was the one who acted for the good of the world and to renew the old, comforting magic in the name of her god. He guided her, gave her the strength she needed to compete the ritual, and compelled her.

An invisible force moved about the room, a heavy presence, as if the Composer had come down to examine his creation's work Himself. It stopped in front of her, the temperature dropping with its presence, and considered her in its stillness. It hummed softly in a low, bass voice that rumbled in her chest. Warmth spread through her, smoothing away her anxiety and lingering protests. A curious pressure built all around her, comforting her as a mother would a child, telling her to stop protesting.

Loretta fell to her knees, her breathing calming with the dying pulse. How silly it was to think that a stained-glass window could have inspired her to take the cloth as a child when the world was so much more wonderfully complex than she could have ever imagined. The ancient glass could not capture this moment, this indescribable feeling of *awe*.

For her god had created this world and everyone in it for a purpose. Resisting the Renewal was futile because it simply could not be done. For as great and terrible as the Renewal was, she felt as if her faith too had been renewed. Slowly, the Music fell into silence, releasing them all from its reassuring embrace until she could hear nothing but her heartbeat in her ears.

The Girl

Maemi Mizunami

Our new house! Shiny painted exterior, beautiful white picket fence, windows so polished you could see the reflections of the clouds in them…is what I'd like to say. Instead, I found myself staring at a broken-down old place, with the picket fence leading to the overgrown garden hanging off its hinges, the paint peeling off the walls, and windows covered in dust and grime. I narrowed my eyes at it, as if that would somehow clean the place up a bit.

Mom called from where she was unpacking the car, "What are you standing there for, Maya? Come and help."

I definitely did not want to help her move into this place. It didn't even look like it would be possible to live here. Why did I have to spend the last two years of high school living in this creepy house? It didn't even deserve to call itself a house.

The curtains in the windows of one of the rooms on the second floor shifted slightly. A shadow appeared there, but then I blinked and it vanished. I shivered involuntarily as I continued to stare at the house.

"Mom, can't we live somewhere else?" I begged. "This place gives me the creeps."

"What do you mean?" Mom glanced briefly at it. "It is a fixer-upper, but you'll see. We can remodel it how we like, and it was a steal. Housing in this area is hard to come by, you know."

I bit my lip, and my mom added, "It'll feel like home in no time. You'll see."

"You sure about that?"

As I continued to look at the house, I suddenly felt a chill come over me. Why did I feel cold in the middle of summer? Sweat covered me from head to toe, and yet I suddenly wanted to put on a jacket. I rubbed my hands along my arms and turned away.

"Maya, catch." Mom tossed me something, and I heard a jangling noise. I caught it and stared at it—a single silver key on a ring.

"Open it up so we can start moving stuff in." Mom looked pointedly at the moving van behind me, where a couple of movers were setting up the ramp in preparation for bringing our furniture and belongings out of the van.

I trudged up the front steps, pausing as the top one creaked slightly under my weight. Add that to the list of things my mom would need to fix.

The dark maroon front door loomed out at me. I stuck the key in the lock and turned it, letting out a little sigh of relief as it clicked and the door opened.

Inside, everything was covered in dust. A slight breeze kicked up from behind me, stirring up the dust on the floor. I sneezed.

My mom came up the stairs and stood next to me. "Wow, this is dustier than I thought it would be! The estate manager said he'd sent someone to clean up a bit yesterday. Guess that didn't happen."

The darkness beckoned to me, as if it wanted me to go further inside. The wind pushed at my back. It was as if I was being ushered inside. I glanced at the walls nearby, looking for a light switch, but the closest one was a few steps away at the foot of the stairs.

"Mom, can you turn on the light?" I stepped back a bit from the door. "This place gives me the creeps."

My mom raised an eyebrow at me. "What do you mean? You've been acting weird ever since we got here."

"Please, Mom." I begged.

My mom rolled her eyes at me, but she stepped inside and flicked on the lights. "See? Nothing to be scared of."

I looked again. The lights illuminated the dust on the floor and alleviated some of the creep factor, but I still didn't feel any better.

"Why don't you go upstairs and see your room?" Mom suggested. "It's the one with the blue carpet. That way, you can figure out how you want things arranged before the movers bring your bed in."

Right. Living in an actual house meant I'd get my own room! After the divorce, we'd moved into a tiny apartment, and my room had been little more than a closet. More often than not, it had also been taken over by Mom's various quilting projects. Now that Mom had a new job and we could live in an actual house again, I could have a bigger room. Maybe it wouldn't be so bad living out here in the suburbs, after all.

The second floor had a bathroom right at the top of the stairs. I took a peek in there, and it actually looked pretty nice. The linoleum floor shone a bit under the light as I flicked on the switch, and the toilet and shower looked pretty clean.

Down the hall from the bathroom were four bedrooms, two more than we needed. We could easily reserve one for guests, and Mom would have an extra room for all her quilting supplies. No more sleeping surrounded by scraps of cloth with the sewing machine as a roommate!

The first three rooms off the hall were all hardwood floors. Guess mine was at the end of the hall.

I opened the door. A huge room, more than twice the size of the one I'd had in our old apartment. Even if we brought in my bed, desk, and the bookshelf I'd had since I was a baby, there would still be plenty of room. But then I did a double-take.

The shadow that I saw flashed again by the window, and something I couldn't see brushed past me. The wind?

I crossed the room and opened the curtain. The window was closed.

But as I turned around, something right in front of the closet caught my eye. It was a dark stain, bigger than my foot, and almost completely circular. What was it? I stared at it for another minute or so before realizing what it was.

It was blood.

***

I don't remember calling for her, but my mom came bounding up the stairs, and then I felt her hand on my shoulder.

I couldn't say anything. I felt like my throat was shut tight. So I waited for her to say something. Surely she would agree—we couldn't stay here now.

"What's wrong with you?" Mom turned a critical gaze on me, her eyebrow raised in the way it sometimes did when she thought I was overreacting. "Is there something wrong, Maya?"

Could it be that Mom couldn't see the stain? I rubbed my eyes. Were they starting to go bad or something? Maybe it was just my imagination.

But the stain was still there. The blood looked old, and I couldn't smell it. I glanced at her.

"The stain…" I gulped out.

Mom furrowed her brows and examined the carpet. "I don't see anything wrong with it."

"But… You don't see it? There's a bloodstain right there!"

Mom shook her head.

"Maybe we could get rid of the carpet?" I suggested hopefully.

She thought for a minute. "It's such a lovely color, and the estate manager says it was installed only recently. It would be such a shame to get rid of it."

"Can I use another bedroom, instead?" I begged.

"Well, I don't see why not. Though you are being a bit silly."

She turned as the movers came up the stairs with my bed frame. "Sorry, that goes in the other bedroom." She directed them to put it in the room next door.

I gladly followed the movers into the other room. No shadows, no bloodstains. It would have to do.

"Wait." I stopped them as they made to put the bed frame against the wall opposite the blue bedroom. "Put it on the other side, instead."

The two college-aged guys glanced at each other, shrugged, and set the bed against the wall farthest from the blue bedroom. As they left to go get the next load, I heard one of them scoff under his breath to his friend, "Picky one, isn't she?"

"You're still being silly," Mom insisted from the doorway. "There's nothing wrong with that room."

But I didn't care. I couldn't stand to be in that room.

It took most of the afternoon, but finally all our belongings were moved in. I had been looking forward to unpacking the boxes and setting up my new room, but I needed to get out of that house, because the longer I stayed there, the more creeped-out I felt. It was as if someone other than the two of us was there. So when Mom asked me to walk down to the corner grocery for some milk and a few other things, I immediately said yes.

Leaving my mom to make a phone call, I ambled down the street, not at all in a rush to do the shopping or go back home again. I strolled through our new neighborhood, admiring the houses I passed and lamenting how we got the one awful one in the entire neighborhood.

And the stain from earlier continued to bug me. Why hadn't my mom been able to see it? Was I going crazy? Had I simply imagined it? Maybe I had freaked myself out so much that I had convinced myself that there was a stain there. Yeah, that had to be it. There's no way there could have been a stain.

I had just convinced myself of this when I came upon a park. A winding path cut through trees and grass, leading to a playground with colorful equipment. The shaded areas of the park were full of kids playing soccer or tag, and a few young mothers all sat together at a picnic table in the shade, but it being almost ninety degrees out, the un-shaded playground was basically empty.

Weird. I suddenly got an overwhelming sense of deja vu looking at that park. Even though I hadn't been to a park in a while. Our last apartment was smack in the middle of the city, nowhere near a park.

Then I noticed the little girl who sat on the swing, staring at the ground.

Her long strawberry-blond hair was matted and dirty, and her jeans had holes in them. She gently kicked the swing back and forth, but the metal chains didn't make a single noise as the links clanked against each other. Aside from her unkempt appearance, there didn't seem to be anything else strange about her. But then she raised her head, and I saw the blood spattered on her shirt.

She stared straight at me, her face blank and expressionless. It seemed as if she was studying me. The entire time she looked at me, I couldn't move. My feet felt stuck to the ground, like they were being sucked into mud or something. Then she blinked, and I was freed from whatever had held me in place. What was that just now? Why hadn't I been able to move?

The girl still watched me, tipping her head to one side. I suddenly felt the urge to walk toward her, and I took a few steps along the path. Her eyes never left me.

I took several more steps. I didn't want to get closer to her. I wanted to run far away. But it was as if something was pulling me toward her, like a chain around my waist.

As I walked through the low fence that surrounded the playground, she suddenly vanished. I stood still for a moment, staring at the swings where she had been. If she'd been sitting on it and gotten off again, the swing would be moving just a bit…but it wasn't.

I shivered and jogged out of that park as fast as I possibly could. Even the kids playing soccer on the grassy field seemed off somehow.

Wait, where was I? I was fairly certain I had memorized where I had come from, but now it was as if I had gotten turned around. I didn't know my way back to our new house. I walked down the street for a while, but nothing looked familiar. And the entire time, I got the impression that I was being followed.

I glanced surreptitiously over my shoulder. That same girl was walking behind me, keeping a good distance between us. I wondered if I should help her somehow.

The girl stopped when she noticed me looking at her. "You're lost, right? The corner grocery is over that way."

She pointed. "Take a right down the next street and then walk four blocks. Then turn left."

Her speech seemed a little stilted, almost monotone. Before I could muster more than a quick "thanks," she had turned around and walked the opposite way, back toward the park.

The feeling of unease continued to grow in my stomach.

Walking as fast as I could, I followed her instructions—right, four blocks, left—and then saw ahead of me the neon sign for "Smith Corner Grocery." I stepped gratefully through the sliding glass doors. The air conditioning surrounded me, but I welcomed it less for its relief from the unforgiving summer heat than from the shivers that continued to creep down my spine. This was a welcoming, familiar cold, and I stood in front of the milk fridge for a minute just to be able to enjoy it.

"You took a long time," my mom remarked as she stood in the living room surrounded by stacks of boxes.

"Sorry about that. I got a bit lost."

"No need to apologize." Mom shrugged and opened one of the boxes on top. "Go ahead and put those groceries away. The movers have already put everything in your room, so all that's left is for you to unpack and organize how you like."

"Thanks." I started for the kitchen but then hesitated. "What about the rug in the other room?"

"Hm?" Mom took out some books from her box and put them on the bookshelf. "Oh, someone will come tomorrow to professionally steam-clean it. Is that okay?"

No, that wasn't okay. I wanted that rug gone. But I didn't want to make too big of a deal out of it, especially since Mom was so excited about this house. So I just nodded and went to the kitchen.

I put away the groceries and spent the rest of the evening trying to concentrate on cleaning and arranging my room, but was constantly distracted. I kept hearing voices from the other room—a woman comforting what I thought was a little girl sobbing. But every time I went into the hallway, it stopped. And at one point, I wandered downstairs to find my mom had the TV on to a channel with a child crying softly in the background, and a woman's voice talking over her.

Just my imagination.

I kept trying to remind myself of that and managed to get enough of my things put away so that I didn't feel like I'd wasted the entire afternoon. Mom and I had some delivery pizza for dinner, and I went to bed. But I couldn't sleep. Every time I closed my eyes, I heard the blood-curdling scream of a girl that faded as quickly as it had come.

What was happening to me? Was I going crazy or something? I lay on my back and stared at the ceiling. Unlike earlier, I no longer heard the woman comforting the crying child. So was this scream-thing also just my imagination?

At one point, I got up and went over to my desk to pick up my phone. The display read 3:41 AM.

Standing at my desk, I closed my eyes, and immediately, that scream filled my ears again.

I padded downstairs, but everything was dark. Mom wasn't watching late-night TV like she sometimes did. What the heck was going on?

***

The next morning, my mom was already in the kitchen by the time I went downstairs.

"Wow, you look awful." She poured herself some coffee and took a sip. "Couldn't sleep?"

I nodded, not having the energy to say anything. Casting my eyes at her fashionable navy blazer and slacks, I muttered, "Off to work?"

"Yeah. I would have liked a few more days to settle in, but they wanted me to start today." She grabbed her purse from the counter and added, "The carpet guy will be here at ten, so can you be sure to be home around that time?" She opened her wallet and counted out three twenties, adding, "This should be enough to pay him. If it turns out to be more, just pay him back from your allowance and I'll reimburse you."

She waved to me from the front door as she left. I glanced around, wondering what there was in terms of breakfast. It was too hot out to make a proper meal. I zapped some leftover pizza in the microwave and then wandered upstairs to get dressed.

Just past eleven, the doorbell rang, and I opened it to see a middle-aged guy wearing a jacket with the logo for a carpet cleaning company. I showed him the room upstairs with the blue carpet, and as he set about to his work, I casually mentioned that the stain in the carpet was the reason we were getting it cleaned.

"I don't see a stain," the guy replied. "But it's dusty in here, so this carpet should get a deep clean."

Was it truly my imagination, then? Was I just going crazy? I stared at the tiny balcony outside the window for a second and then went to my room next door while he worked.

He finished and dragged his equipment back out to his truck. When I asked him how much it would cost, he said fifty. So I wound up with a ten-dollar bill and nothing to do on a hot summer day.

I decided to take a stroll down to the grocery store and get some ice cream or something with the change. The blazing sun warmed my bare arms and face, and the fresh air woke me up somewhat.

I got a pint of Neapolitan ice cream—Mom's favorite—and started home.

I was about five blocks away from home when I saw her again. The same girl from before, following me. She still wore the same bloodstained t-shirt, and her matted blond hair was still dirty and unwashed. Why did she seem so familiar to me when I'd only met her yesterday?

I crossed the street, and she followed me. A car came almost from out of nowhere and zoomed toward her, missing her by only an inch.

My heart pounded in my ears. I jogged over to her. "Hey, are you all right? That car almost hit you. You're not hurt or anything, are you?"

She shook her head. "No, I'm okay. Nothing hurts me anymore."

"I… I saw you yesterday, didn't I? At the park?"

She inclined her chin.

"Are you hurt or something? There's blood all over your shirt."

"No." The girl paused. "It's old. I'm all better now."

"I see." I took a breath to try and calm down. "Are your parents around here? Want me to walk you home?"

"My parents…are at the house," she replied. "I can get home on my own."

Unsure of what else to say, I started back down the street. "Well, I'm glad you're not hurt. See you later."

She followed me for another three blocks. I started to get annoyed.

I stopped and turned on one heel to face her, opening my mouth to tell her to stop following me. She stood just out of arm's reach, staring at me with accusatory eyes.

"I'm not following you. That's where I live."

She pointed. Her index finger unmistakably indicated our "fixer-upper" house.

"You don't live there," I replied. "That's my house."

The girl shook her head, her firm gaze not leaving me for an instant. "It *is* my house. I live there with my parents. My carpet is blue, like the ocean."

I stared at her for a minute.

She lowered her arm. "I have to go now. Bye."

And then she turned and vanished down a side street.

I continued absentmindedly toward our house, not sure of what to think.

I let myself into the house and started up the stairs before remembering that I was carrying a plastic bag with ice cream. I had forgotten it was in my hand.

I put the carton of ice cream in the freezer, not really in the mood anymore for a treat. Then I wandered upstairs again, thinking that I might as well finish cleaning up my room so I didn't have to worry about it when school started next week.

The door at the end of the hall was open just a crack. I stopped at the top of the stairs. I closed it after the carpet guy left, didn't I?

I stopped outside my bedroom. Some compulsion within me told me to open the door to that room.

I took slow, reluctant steps toward it. Why was I so afraid? I'd been in that room only a little while ago, when the carpet guy was working in there.

The handle of the door was cold underneath my fingers. Part of me wanted to open it, just to prove that it was an empty room and there was nothing to be afraid of. Part of me wanted to run back downstairs, turn on the TV, the computer, the lights. Anything to make this unease go away. But the part of me that felt as if it was being called by whatever was beyond that door was stronger. It won.

I turned the handle slowly, determined to prove to myself that there was nothing there. But then the door swung open, and my breath caught in my throat.

The girl from earlier stood on the balcony outside the window, staring at me, her nose pressed up against the glass. A shriek escaped my throat.

She noticed me and stepped away from the window. I was frozen in place. My feet wouldn't move. Who was this girl?

She pointed to the lock on the window. I wanted to run away, but my feet carried me toward her. Dread filling my heart, I opened the window just a crack.

"Wh—" My throat felt dry. I coughed to clear it. "What do you want?"

"I wanted to see my room one more time."

She glanced at the floor and sighed. "There's no carpet. I guess it really isn't my house."

No carpet? But…there was, right?

"How did you get up there?" I asked.

She blinked at me. "I can fly."

She took one step backward. I reached out the window to stop her, but my hand only grabbed the air. My breath caught. She was gone, but there was no broken, bloody body in the garden below. Someone want to explain to me what's going on here?

I ran back to my room and grabbed my phone, unsure of what I was even going to do. Maybe I just wanted to tell someone else about what I had seen. My mom? My friends? I jumped on Facebook and was almost about to post a status update about it. But then something stopped me from doing so. I suddenly got the urge to access the local newspaper archives online.

An article from a few years ago caught my eye. Two parents in the neighborhood had committed suicide after their daughter died. The police investigation found evidence that they had been hitting their daughter for a while—the teacher at school had noticed bruises on her arms and way more cuts and scrapes than would be normal for a kid. The police thought the parents killed the daughter, but the autopsy was inconclusive.

My mom didn't believe me when I told her about the screams, even though they continued for years. I didn't get another good night's sleep until I went away to college.

I never saw the girl again.

SHIP
DESERTED

Sargasso 1840

Renée Harvey

Inspired by the true story of the merchant vessel, Rosalie, *which sailed from Brest, France, in 1840.*

***

Captain's log: July 8, 1840. Good progress made today. Wind speed remains a constant six knots. Yesterday's storm seems to have cleared. Another few days and we should be far enough south to avoid the *sargassum*-covered doldrums across this part of the Atlantic. Arrival at New Orleans predicted for the first week of August. Passengers and crew in high spirits.

***

Éloïse Blanchard gripped the *Rosalie*'s wooden rail as the wind tossed her stray hair and gown about. She planted her feet surely on the deck as she looked over the wide blue-green ocean. Waves broke against the vessel's bow, casting light, salty sprays across her face every now and again. The sails above her, full of air, billowed as they pushed the ship ever farther away from France. Éloïse didn't look back; she looked forward.

She imagined she could already see the New World's legendary forested shores surrounding the New Orleans harbor. There, she would take up residence with her sister until her husband, Captain Luc Blanchard, had saved enough money from his sailing ventures to purchase their own property. The whole idea filled Éloïse with an anticipation that made her fingers and toes tingle.

Meow. Fifi nuzzled her ankles, eager for attention.

"Oh, *mon chaton,* what are you doing outside our quarters?" Éloïse scooped up the sleek black cat as she backed away from the edge. "Don't you realize there is nothing to catch you if you go over that rail?" She nuzzled her face in the cat's fur. "Besides," she whispered, "if you jump, the crew will likely send me in after you." She shuddered. She couldn't swim well, and the crew was eager to get rid of the bad luck her very presence brought to this vessel.

Not that there had been any streak of bad luck that Éloïse had seen, but who could argue with the logic of half a dozen sailors responsible for seeing her safely to New Orleans? Especially when one of those men was her husband's mammoth first mate, Armand.

Éloïse shuddered again and buried her face in Fifi's soft fur.

"Mothering the cat again, are you?" her husband asked, and Éloïse turned. Luc wore an amused smile on that unshaven face of his. He had left his captain's coat elsewhere; his cotton shirt was casually tucked into his trousers, and his worn blue boots scuffed against the freshly cleaned deck.

"So what if I am?" Éloïse remarked as she made a show of petting Fifi's head. The cat's purr vibrated through her hand.

Luc chuckled. He squinted as he leaned against the rail, scanning the ocean.

"What are you looking for?" Éloïse asked. She hadn't seen much wildlife since the whales spouted a few hours ago, and Luc always checked the chronometer with Armand.

She frowned at Luc's hunched posture. "*Mon destin*, is it another headache?" She let Fifi jump down to the deck and rested her hand on Luc's shoulder. A hint of panic fluttered through her as she saw his eyes closed tight and his jawline tense, but he gave her a brief smile.

"It's nothing, *ma colombe*. Don't worry about it."

Éloïse *would* worry about it. Her father was a physician; some things she just couldn't ignore. She brushed Luc's long hair off his forehead. "Didn't Cook's tonic help last time?"

Luc shrugged. "There is not much of it left. Others need it more than me."

"Others more than the captain who will be seeing them safely all the way across the Atlantic?" Éloïse huffed. "Luc, you really must learn to think more highly of yourself. Go ask Cook for the tonic."

"And miss out on a rare few moments with my wife?" Luc retorted with a gleam in his eye. "*Non, Madame.*"

Éloïse put her hands to her hips in complaint, but running footsteps from behind interrupted her argument.

"Captain!" one of the seamen shouted, coming up the stairs.

Luc frowned. "What is it, Jacques?"

"It's Gilbert, sir," Jacques said, panting, a hand on his knee. His ponytail was loose, pulled to the side of his head like he'd gotten into a tussle with Fifi. "He's convulsing, raving like a madman."

Luc ran after Jacques in an instant, and Éloïse followed, lifting her skirts to avoid tripping as her heart began to beat fast. Convulsions weren't a good sign, especially with the ship's boatswain. Convulsions were always a symptom of a much larger problem, and Luc had spent too many months seeking a man who actually knew how to repair a large merchant ship like this. Éloïse prayed that whatever had caused this fit would pass soon. The crew would likely blame her for Gilbert's condition, threatening her with being thrown overboard until he healed.

Below deck, Luc followed Jacques into a storeroom, but Armand blocked Éloïse from following. "This is not the place for a woman, *Madame*," he stated, standing in front of the open entryway with a hard expression. "Cook will take care of him."

"Even a woman with my knowledge?" Éloïse complained. Her heart ached as a pained shout came from the dark room. Gilbert avoided her, same as all the others, but at least when she happened to be in the same place as him, he wasn't rude about it like the other sailors were.

"Make them stop!" Gilbert cried from within the dark room.

"No, hold him tight," Cook commanded.

"The beetles. The beetles, make them go away!"

"There are no bugs. We're in the middle of the ocean," Cook retorted.

Another anguished scream reverberated off the wooden bulkheads and tugged at Éloïse's heartstrings. "I can help him, sir."

Armand shook his head. His thick tree-trunk body prevented her from catching a glimpse of Gilbert, Luc, or even Cook with him.

"Isn't there something you can give him?" Luc demanded. "Something to quiet him?"

"I sent one of the boys for my tonics, Captain," Cook replied. "He'll be back in a minute."

A sudden lanky shadow appeared next to Éloïse, making her jump out of her skin.

Armand moved aside just enough for a teen boy to slip under his arm with a small drawstring bag in hand. Something clanked within.

"Careful, boy," Cook said. "Let's see what's in here."

Éloïse tapped her foot impatiently. She knew what tonics to use to calm convulsions. Mugwort would do some good, perhaps castor oil if needed. She could administer them, and surely Cook had been wise enough to at least bring plenty of mugwort aboard.

Though perhaps it wasn't convulsions that were the problem, but the ravings Éloïse heard. What beetles?

Gilbert's cries quieted to whispers, but still Armand remained unmoving in front of the door. Éloïse huffed and turned down the corridor to go to her quarters. If she wouldn't be allowed in to see Gilbert, at the very least she could begin researching what might be the cause of his illness. She would put her father's books to good use.

***

"Find her," one of the seamen growled from outside the cargo room door. "Find her, and cast her to the waves."

"But the captain," another protested.

Éloïse hunched farther into her corner of the cargo room, shoulders scrunched as she tried to make herself smaller in the shadows.

"He needs a boatswain more than a wife," the first grumbled. "If she can curse Gilbert, we'll all be next."

The man's voice faded as he drifted away from the room, and Éloïse dared to breathe. Half a dozen medical journals were stacked beside her with a roll from the galley resting on top of the pile. Her growling stomach chastised her for not grabbing a second roll, but the men in the corridors had convinced her being hungry was a small price to pay.

Crates filled with beautiful material, wines, and other goods were stacked all around her, effectively hiding her from a straight view of the door. She sat on one crate headed for New Orleans, and the two on either side of her were destined for Havannah. Master Raoul had staked quite a bit of his fortune in providing the owners of the Cuban plantations with all the luxuries their money could buy.

The occasional rustle of pigs' feet or cluck of a chicken from the livestock hold next door were the only sounds Éloïse could hear. It was eerie, knowing the ship carried a good handful of crew members as well as the merchants, and yet it was all quiet.

At least she would hear if someone approached her.

Or if Fifi decided to try again to steal milk from the cow. The last attempt had ended with a faint hoof imprint in Fifi's fur.

Éloïse relit her lamp. The flare momentarily blinded her. She blinked away blue and purple spots but winced as a headache wormed its way to the front of her head. It faded soon enough, and she took a bite of the sweet roll as she opened the first journal, intent on discovering the cure for Gilbert so she could navigate the corridors in peace.

How to cure ailments of the skin…
How to cure ailments of the digestive tract…
How to cure ailments of the mind…

Éloïse continued to skim the pages, snacking on her roll until the entire thing was reduced to cream-and-black crumbs that she brushed off her skirt and onto the crate. Little help seemed to be contained in these pages. Éloïse needed to know the cause before she could try to treat it. She tossed the book next to her stack, her gaze straying too close to the bright flame, and the faded headache was rekindled.

Éloïse winced, shielding her eyes from the light. She focused on regulating her breathing until the painful flare faded.

In and out.

In…out.

In…

The headache wasn't fading. Éloïse waited several more minutes with no change.

Taking a breath, and determined not to be cowed, she scooped up her books and lamp, and ventured back through the narrow hallways to her quarters. The headache remained constant, thudding against her head with each footstep on the swaying wooden floor.

"Perhaps I should've stayed for dinner in the galley," she muttered to herself. Too often she got headaches from not eating properly. It served her right, her father would say.

"Please, papa, won't you just give me a little morphine to hold until supper is served?"

Her father wasn't here now, and Cook had already told Luc he had no morphine, but others had complained of headaches, too. Cook had a tonic.

Cook also sided with Armand and the others in their objection to having Éloïse on board, no matter how benign Luc tried to convince them she was. Cook would never give her the precious tonic.

Neither would he acquiesce to her eating after dinner had already ended.

Éloïse's stomach cramped painfully, and she gripped her midsection, anticipating the growl, but it never came. It must be a menstrual cramp.

One that would've been mitigated had she simply eaten at dinner.

Wishing she really could put a blinding hex on the men, or a transformation spell on herself, Éloïse entered her quarters, tossed the books on the desk just inside the door, and allowed herself an undignified flop onto the feather bed. The heavy woven fabric felt cool on her skin. Her canaries twittered in their cage by the window. The *peck-peck* of seeds hitting the floor created a soft lullaby that flowed with the gentle sway of the ship.

***

Captain's Log: July 15, 1840. Progress was poorer today. Wind slowed to three knots. Will need to watch for storms, and must remember to check the chronometer tomorrow. We are certainly headed west instead of south, and there have been no sightings of *sargassum*. We're past the doldrums.

***

"Ugh," Éloïse groaned as she leaned over the ship's railing with her stomach tied in painful knots. "Of course Luc would insist the fresh, salty air would do me good, and of course I would think to listen to him."

The sun felt too hot on her long sleeves. The dingy fabric felt sticky on her skin. Her hair, quickly wound into a bun, felt heavy on her head, which continued to throb. It was a constant pounding centered between her left eye and ear, with heat radiating all through her head. Only sleep seemed to free her from the aching. Sleep, and fruit from the ship's stores. The rolls and gruel were more filling, and she knew she needed the nourishment, but somehow they just seemed to make her headache worse.

It must be the lack of proper vegetables and protein. The entire crew had these headaches, as did the merchants, but if it was something about their diet, there was nothing that could be done about it until they reached New Orleans. Luc had never mentioned this constant sickness when he talked about his seafaring adventures. Had he simply learned to live with it?

Fifi purred as he rubbed against Éloïse's leg, but she didn't have the strength to bend down and pet his silky fur. "Not now, Fifi."

Fifi yowled and scampered off. Éloïse groaned. The sooner they made it to New Orleans, the better everyone would be. The men complained about how Cook's tonic had run out the other day. Gilbert was still in isolation on a diet of gruel to help him keep his strength up. Cook had forbidden Éloïse from attending to him, but that didn't stop her from hearing the many pained and delirious screams. In what seemed to be moments free of torment, she heard Gilbert shout about the beetles, and at other times, he seemed to delve into madness.

"Ponies!" he had chortled the other day. "What beautifully plaited tails!"

If Éloïse had the strength, she would have scoured every one of her books by now for a definitive answer as to what was ailing the crew. Typhoid fever was possible, or perhaps gonorrhea. She shuddered as she recalled that the Plague also had similar symptoms to what the crew was experiencing, then turned her hands over and over, checking for boils.

"Land ho!" Alain shouted from the crow's nest.

Éloïse looked up to where he was pointing across the clear blue waves. The others clambered to the far side of the rail. Éloïse squinted against the sun as she instinctively braced herself for defense.

If she stared hard enough across the crystal blue waves, she could detect something brown in the distance. An island, perhaps, very near sea level. Luc would want to chart it.

"Let's get the wind in these sails!" Armand called out, prompting another scampering of feet against the deck. "*Madame*, will you *please* get below?"

Swallowing her frustrations at being ordered around like chattel, Éloïse headed away from the rail, arms clenched tight around her midsection. Above her, the unfurled sails barely puffed. No moving air to make this heat more bearable, or to push the *Rosalie* closer to New Orleans. She descended below deck, sidestepping a chicken that had gotten loose from the cargo room. Hopefully someone would put it back in its cage before Fifi found it.

Coming around a corner, she bumped into Luc. "Oh, *mon destin!*"

He caught her, letting her rest against his chest for a moment. "*Ma colombe*, did you get enough air?"

She nodded then blinked, recalling what had sent her back down. "Alain has spotted an island. Armand is headed straight for it." She smiled. "Wouldn't it be wonderful to have a day or two on land before continuing on to New Orleans?"

"An island?" Luc asked. She heard the incredulity in his sharp tone. "We're in the middle of the Atlantic, Éloïse. Are you sure your brain hasn't been addled with all your sleeping?"

She pushed away from him, resisting the urge to hold her forehead as the movement made her wince from a sudden throb. "It must be yours that's addled to not believe your own wife."

He cringed and headed toward the ladder. Éloïse returned to their quarters. Out of habit, she kept one hand on the wall for balance, but the floorboards beneath her feet seemed steadier than they had in weeks. How strange it felt to not have to wonder how far down to step to reach the deck bobbing under her. At least the sea was kind to her headache today.

She crawled back into bed, groaning as her canaries started their whistling, and covered her head with her blanket. She must have dozed, because the next thing she was aware of was Luc curling up beside her.

"Did you see the island?" she mumbled, her voice hoarse.

Luc massaged her arm. Perhaps he didn't understand her gravelly words.

"Luc, will we stop at the island?" she asked again, speaking a little clearer this time.

His hand on her arm slowed. "*Ma colombe*, it wasn't an island. I told you, we're in the middle of the Atlantic."

"But Alain said—" She rolled over to look at Luc, squinting in the dim light. "Did Alain not say there was land ahead?"

Luc stared across the room. "He was mistaken, *ma colombe*."

Éloïse chuckled. "You did not hire him to be mistaken, *mon destin*."

"Nevertheless, what he saw was merely a thick patch of *sargassum*." Luc sounded bitter, and Éloïse squinted at him, not understanding.

"What is *sargassum*?"

Luc got up and started pacing. "It's a seaweed. It's brown, and drifts over a certain part of the ocean. Columbus mentioned it in his logs."

"But doesn't seaweed mean we're close to land?" Éloïse pushed away her covers, briefly relishing in the cooler air above the blankets.

Luc shook his head. "Not this time. The seaweed, the heat, the extra saltiness and pure blue of the water, the lack of wind—" He paused and rubbed his neck. "I thought we were farther south. I thought we'd avoided this part of the ocean…"

Éloïse swallowed, fighting against the dull ache in her head. "Luc, you're rambling. What is it?"

He stopped in the middle of the floor. Hesitantly, he looked back to her, his solemn green eyes full of apology.

She wasn't going to like what he would say. Was it too late to take back her words, to remain ignorant?

"We've entered the doldrums, Éloïse. We're not going anywhere anytime soon."

***

Master Antoine's horse whinnied. Its panicked hooves stomped on the deck. The vibrations reached all the way to Éloïse, who stood with eyes squeezed closed in the shadows of the wheel. She clutched Fifi tightly, stroking the black cat, and praying the action would free some of the good luck he supposedly brought to the ship. She didn't want to be thrown overboard, too.

"Come on, men, hold him steady!"

The horse protested further, and Éloïse imagined him straining against the ropes that had been used to lead him above deck and away from his safe cargo hold. She couldn't watch, but neither could she remain in her cabin so close to the other stamping, bleating livestock. It was as if they sensed they were headed to slaughter.

"Steady now!"

Éloïse's heart leaped to her throat.

The horse's next whinny was cut short.

Moments later, there was a heavy splash.

Éloïse released a shaky breath and continued furiously stroking Fifi, who clung to her arm, his nails biting Éloïse's skin.

The heaviest of items had to go overboard. "Lighten the ship" had been Luc's orders. "Get rid of everything we don't need, anything weighing us down."

The horses had to go, the cow and all the feed had to go. The crew's stocks of wines and meat had to go.

Cook had argued for half the chickens to stay. "The eggs will sustain us to port."

The oranges could stay, but the apples had cascaded into the deep blue waves. The potatoes followed soon after—bag upon bag of them plunking into the water and disappearing into the bottomless depths. Food meant to feed Éloïse and the crew.

Cook saved the flour. Oranges and flour, and the occasional egg to feed everyone all the way to New Orleans. It was a good thing Éloïse had already lost most of her appetite thanks to her constant, nagging headache.

The cow's moo sounded from below. Led by other crewmen, she clopped up the stairs and onto the deck. Each footfall felt like a second heartbeat in Éloïse's feet.

That was Conrad's cow. The second mate had meant to put her on a parcel of land once they got to New Orleans to start his homestead.

The cow protested the slaughter, requiring what sounded like three sailors to hold her still. Her trampling made the deck vibrate. Éloïse leaned back against the bulkhead, clutching tightly to Fifi. There was a final cry from the animal, then silence, and a heavy splash into the sea.

Fifi yowled. Éloïse held her close.

"No, *mon chaton*, they won't send you overboard." Éloïse had no such guarantee, captain's wife or no. If she stayed in the shadows, perhaps they wouldn't see her.

"Armand, I told you, we keep the goods."

At the sound of Luc's voice, Éloïse opened her eyes.

Her husband led the way on deck, his shirt sleeves rolled up past his elbows, his stride tense. Armand stomped up behind him, his burly features angry red.

"Half the load, Captain. That's all I'm asking. We have to lighten the ship if we're going to make use of any breeze we might catch."

"And whose half do you propose we dump?" Luc demanded as he headed for the stairway to the wheel. "Master Sebastien's? Master Raoul's?" He paused midway up and snapped his fingers. "I know, Master—"

"Captain, I must speak with you!"

"Antoine's," Luc finished, hardening his gaze as the third merchant, richly dressed in ruffles and coat, strode up to him. Antoine was the only one who insisted on dressing in all his best attire, even so far from port.

Armand pounded his fist against the rail. Antoine had paid the highest prices of all the merchants to ship his goods: crates of silks and fine wines, some of the best available in all of Brittany.

"Captain, my horse?" Antoine stopped at the base of the steps, and wiped his forehead with a dingy handkerchief. "You had no right, sir. That beast was my property!"

"It was either the horse, or your wines, sir," Luc retorted. "You can purchase another one after your wares are sold."

"Ah, so you will be keeping the merchandise?" Antoine clarified, puffing out his chest a bit. "And what of the goods belonging to Raoul and Sebastien?"

Luc looked pointedly at Armand.

"We'll keep them all," Armand muttered, and Luc dismissed him with a sharp hand wave. Armand sidestepped the pigs Jacques and Alain were bringing up from below, then disappeared back downstairs. Éloïse sighed in relief.

The heavy pigs grunted as the seamen tugged on their ropes.

"Are you sure we can't convince Cook to let us keep one for the bacon?" Alain asked with a hungry look on his face.

Jacques laughed, but his pig bolted, sprinting across the deck faster than Éloïse had known was possible.

"Hey! Stop him!" Jacques's call for help was echoed across the deck as Conrad and the boys raced after the creature. It squealed as it reached the far rail, then darted to the side, and squealed even louder when one of the boys slammed into it.

The pig struggled against his grip, twisting this way and that in a valiant effort to escape. Éloïse covered Fifi's eyes, her own heart beating heavily.

Conrad helped the boy wrestle the pig still. Jacques took a firm grip on the rope.

"Just get it done," Conrad demanded, and Jacques pulled out a long silver knife that gleamed in the sun.

Éloïse closed her eyes, turning away as the pig's final cries were silenced. Then, there was another splash in the waves. The second pig quickly followed, and Éloïse suddenly felt very hot. Her stomach clenched. She heaved.

"There," she heard Jacques say with a tinge of regret. "No more bacon."

Fifi leaped out of her arms just in time for Éloïse to double over. Vomit, hot and acidic, splashed against the deck and onto her hem.

Luc was at her side in an instant as she coughed up the remains.

"*Ma colombe*, what are you doing out here? I thought you were resting below deck."

"How could I?" she asked, wiping her mouth with her dingy rose sleeve. "The animals were causing too much of a ruckus."

He gave her a sympathetic smile. "The animals won't bother you now. You should go lay down."

Éloïse glared before sagging back against the bulkhead. The only reason the animals would be silent was because they were *gone*. All save her canaries, a handful of chickens, and Fifi.

Her cat stood a few paces away, his bristled tail flicking as he watched the seamen, who now eyed Éloïse with accusatory glares.

Trembling, she reached out her hand. "Come, Fifi. We'll go below." Scooping him, she made for the stairs. Someone touched her arm, and she jumped.

It was just Luc.

"Let me help you," he said, wincing. That was his headache again.

She shook her head. "No. Stay here, Captain, and see us to New Orleans." The sooner, the better.

***

Captain's Log: July, 21 1840. The wind picked up to a generous knot this afternoon. Crew and passengers had rations of bread, water, and oranges today. So bland compared to the apple pie Cook made yesterday. The steam rose off it with a scent straight from the heavens, and the juices were as sweet as honey. I can still taste it.

***

Cook tossed the plate on the counter, where it rattled before coming to a stop. Éloïse shook off her headache as she took the gruel and orange quarters. She scrutinized Cook, who leaned heavily on the counter, his forehead dotted with perspiration.

"See that the captain eats," he growled.

Éloïse nodded and left the counter, glancing back as she navigated between the tables. The perspiration, the trouble focusing his vision on any one spot, the way Cook rubbed his forehead… He was falling ill, too. How long would it be before the ship lacked both boatswain and cook?

Luc sat at their table, leaned back with his eyes closed.

"*Mon destin*," she murmured, not wanting to disturb him if he was truly asleep.

Luc drew in a sharp breath. He sat up and rubbed his eyes. Éloïse pushed the plate in front of him, then returned to her own seat, where half her orange pieces and much of the thick gruel was already consumed. She stirred the bowl's remaining contents. This was safe to eat; whatever was making everyone ill was surely airborne. Perhaps the hold the livestock had been kept in had not been cleaned well enough.

Luc pulled some of the white off one of his orange slices, lost in his own thoughts. "Cook should've made his apple pie again," he murmured.

"Apple pie?" Éloïse had never had apple pie in Cook's galley.

"Last night's dessert," Luc said matter-of-factly, looking to her as if she was being forgetful.

Éloïse would've remembered having apple pie, but the apples had been tossed into the sea last week. Unless she was wrong, and had somehow forgotten…

She swirled the little black grains around in her cooling gruel and changed the subject. "Have we made any progress?"

Luc shrugged. He popped his orange slice in his mouth. A bit of juice squirted out from his lips. "Some, perhaps, but not enough. We're drifting. The wind refuses to fill our sails."

Éloïse pressed some of her gruel up the side of the bowl to dry and save for her birds. "Is there anything more we can do?"

He sighed then spooned a bite into his mouth. "Our supplies are dwindling, and we've already dumped all we can."

"But the ship is still sound," Éloïse replied. She gestured to the walls. "We have no leaks, and there's nothing wrong with the sails."

"We may as well be in the rowboat," Luc retorted, slamming his fist on the table, where the dishes rattled against the wood. "At least then we could use the oars and actually get to New Orleans!"

Swallowing hard, Éloïse glanced to the boys having their supper in the corner of the room. They had paused at Luc's outburst but quickly turned back to their food. One of them rubbed his stomach with a grimace on his face.

Hunger pains. Éloïse couldn't blame him. Neither could she be angry at Luc. He was never cross with her, but he slept poorly, and there were the headaches that had been plaguing the crew for weeks. She watched Luc swallow the gruel. His eyes were closed in a painful grimace. His shoulder bones were well-defined beneath his limp shirt.

New Orleans would welcome a ship of skeletons at this rate. If only Éloïse could figure out what this illness was!

"Oi!"

Someone shouted from the hall, and there was a rush of footsteps.

"Captain, help!"

Luc jumped up from the table. Bewildered, Éloïse hurried to follow.

In the hall, Luc tackled Armand, who fell on the stairs and dropped several bolts of silky blue cloth.

"Let go of me!" Armand shouted. He kicked Luc away, snagged up one of the bolts, and tried to push past Jacques, who blocked the door to the deck. "Get out of my way!"

"No, sir!" Jacques pushed against the larger Armand with all his might.

Luc hauled the first mate back down the stairs. "Armand, what's the meaning of this? Cook, help!"

Cook pushed past Éloïse and snagged the cloth, thrusting it at her before helping Luc secure Armand's arms behind his back. The first mate's eyes were glazed over, settling on nowhere in particular.

"You don't understand, we're too heavy! We'll drown!" Armand shouted.

"What are you talking about?" Luc asked. He motioned for Éloïse to move out of the way as he and Cook led Armand back down the hall. She hastily picked up the other bolts before following.

Armand wrestled against the men, nearly breaking free of their grips. Éloïse kept herself pressed against the wall, not wanting to be in the big man's way should her husband not be able to hold him.

"No, not below," Armand screeched. "The water! The water's rising, and we're all going to drown!"

The fabric almost slipped through Éloïse's hands. "A leak?"

The men ignored her, continuing to push the struggling first mate down the corridor. She followed, still clutching the bolts. "Luc, that sounds serious."

He silenced her with a sharp glare. "We'll handle him."

Cook called over his shoulder. "Alain, fetch my bag!"

Éloïse watched as the men maneuvered Armand down the hall and into the room where Gilbert still rested.

"No! We must get to the deck! We must lighten the load!"

Cook slammed the door shut. When Alain knocked on the door with the bag of tonics, Cook allowed him to slip in, still blocking Éloïse's view of the interior.

Armand continued to scream. His shouts were just as forceful as his demeanor. The ship was flooding. They had to get rid of the extra cargo. Water. Water everywhere.

Heart thudding in her chest, Éloïse looked around the floor, expecting to see signs of the flooding.

The floors were dry.

The bolts were awkward in Éloïse's arms. She shifted them, and caught a glimpse of something red on the material.

Blood. Splattered and dripping down the bolts, seeping into her dress and onto her sleeves.

She screamed and dropped the bolts, shaking her arms to get rid of the liquid.

"Get off, get off!" She paused and examined the damaged material.

The sleeves were just as clean as they'd been at supper. A couple stains from the orange juice, the pale white fabric looking more yellow thanks to the lack of frequent cleanings. She patted her chest, but the material was damp from her own sweat. The blue material on the floor contained nothing red.

Éloïse exhaled as she leaned against the bulkhead. No blood.

And the floor below her feet remained just as still and level as it had been since entering the doldrums. Hallucinations? Malaria could cause hallucinations.

She hurried back to her room to study, but a sickly smell wafted from the dining area as she approached, making her stomach churn as she gagged.

"Excuse me, *Madame*," the older boy said, gripping his friend under the arms as he came down the hall. The younger lad's face was ashen, and he sagged heavily against the older.

"Is he all right?" she asked.

The older boy shook his head helplessly. "He was fine a few minutes ago."

"Cook is just down the hall." Éloïse led the way. She tried to twist the handle. It wouldn't budge.

"Open up," she demanded, knocking rapidly. "Cook, one of the boys is ill."

Luc opened the door and let the two boys slip by him. He joined Éloïse in the hall, scratching at his unkempt beard.

"What is this voyage coming to?" he muttered. "First mate down, the boy sick, all my crew with headaches and spending more time resting than keeping watch." He roughly scratched his arms.

Éloïse covered his hand with hers to stop him from tearing his skin. "What of Gilbert? He should be on the mend by now."

Luc tugged away from her grip and resumed rubbing his arms. "It'll be a watery grave for him. As soon as Cook has seen to Armand and the boy."

Éloïse stared between him and the door.

Luc met her gaze, his long face solemn. "Gilbert is dead, Éloïse." He rubbed his arms all the harder and whispered, "What if we are all next?"

***

Captain's Log: July 24, 1840. No wind. Nothing to speak of. I walk around this ship, and all I see is death. Shadows of the men I hired for this voyage, weak ghosts wandering about. My wife is one of them. Her eyes are listless, her body weak. The crew will send her off like

Gilbert soon, if they haven't already. And Armand, my best friend and partner. He's the strongest of us all. He has to survive this cursed voyage.

***

Only a few days after Gilbert was sent to the depths of the wide, blue ocean, the sick boy likewise succumbed. Éloïse wanted to cry for him but could manage no more than the tears that fell at the initial shock of receiving the news. Her head hurt like a constant steam train rumbling around in her brain. When she did move, it was slow and deliberate. She stood on the deck after the youth had been cast into the sea, rubbing at her arms. They itched, like ants or pill bugs were tickling her skin.

Of course there are no ants in the ocean, she chided herself, but the itching continued.

At least the breeze was helping her stay cool, a welcome relief from the weeks of near-stagnant humidity. Her skirt furled about her legs, her stringy hair gusted into her face. She closed her eyes, relishing in the cool, fresh, moving air.

Then her eyes snapped open, straight to the sails. They swayed, the heavy fabric popping with the air currents as it had failed to do for so long.

"Look!" she cried, pointing upward and laughing. "The wind! The wind is back!"

Her shouts were echoed all about the ship. The men, too, pointed to the sails, laughing and dancing together.

Luc swept her up, joyfully twirling her around once, before letting her land back on her feet. She winced at the sudden movements but couldn't help but grin at her husband's happy countenance; she gave him the tightest hug she could manage, not caring what the men around them thought, and he hugged her back.

"Tighten the sails!" Conrad called, acting now as first mate.

"Aye, sir!" The sailors jumped to, scurrying about the deck as they hadn't in weeks. The ship seemed to come alive again, and hope filled Éloïse's chest. They would make it to New Orleans!

The sun disappeared behind a cloud, and Éloïse waited for the shade to pass.

The breeze carried with it a damp feeling that clung to her cheeks and dress.

The saltiness of the air faded, replaced with a fresh scent. Rain.

The breeze became wind, the sky grew darker. Thunder rumbled in the distance.

Luc pushed on Éloïse's back. "*Ma colombe,*" he whispered. "Éloïse, go below."

Following Luc's sight, Éloïse gasped.

A wall of dark clouds filled the horizon. Lightning carved a jagged line from cloud to water.

Éloïse called for Fifi as she skittered below deck.

*****

The canaries squawked as their hanging cages rocked back and forth. Fifi yowled from within Éloïse's tight grip, but she refused to let go of her cat. It took all her effort to keep from swaying right into the bulkheads. She sat firmly on her bed, her feet planted solidly on the floor.

Her stomach was not so solid. She closed her eyes, fighting to hold back the bile.

Her room was dark now. The storm had come up so fast, it was as if nighttime had settled on the sea within minutes. She prayerfully pleaded for the storm to cease, for the sea to go back to the gentle calmness it had been for so long.

I'd rather be set adrift again than have to ride out this nightmare of a storm.

The thought made her lose her concentration on holding back the contents of her stomach. She retched. Acid burned her throat and tongue. The disgusting smell filled the cabin, and Fifi scampered away.

"Fifi, no," Éloïse mumbled, wiping her mouth. "We need to stay here where it's safe."

Fifi scratched at the door, yowling. Éloïse moaned. The ship swayed again, tumbling her back on the bed, and the door flew open, slamming against the bulkhead. Éloïse caught a glimpse of her cat's bristled tail escaping out the door.

"Fifi!" Éloïse scrambled up, sidestepped the mess on the floor, and darted to the corridor. She screamed as Armand charged toward her, and dodged out of the way.

Armand gave a guttural yell as he took the steps two at a time and burst through the door to the deck. Rain pelted Éloïse's face, but someone had to stop him. She ran after him, tripping on the top step, catching the slick, wet deck with her hands.

"Armand!" someone else shouted amid the crashing of the waves and rain smacking against the deck.

Éloïse could hardly see. Her wet hair fell across her face. She swiped it away, only to have her vision fill with rainwater as she fell against the pitching deck. Armand appeared as a blur running away from her, straight to the rail.

He gripped the wood and leaped overboard.

"Luc!" she called. "Man overboard!"

The deck pitched, and she toppled over. Her hands and chin smacked the wood. Someone ran by her wearing well-worn blue boots. Luc. She reached for him, but someone else pulled her upright. Alain. She tugged away from him.

Luc reached the spot where Armand had disappeared. He peeled off his coat, tossed it to the deck, and jumped over the rail.

"No!" Éloïse screamed. She scrambled to her feet, pushing Alain away.

Gripping the rail, she peered across the turbulent ocean; the deep waves patched with *sargassum* were sharp and jagged, angry and unforgiving.

"Luc!" she called out, scanning the sea for her husband.

"There!" Alain pointed to the left, and Éloïse caught sight of something that was not foam riding the waves.

A shirt.

Another bobbed to the surface beside it. Luc and Armand!

"Cast them a line!" she begged. A rope went overboard toward the captain and first mate.

"Grab it, grab it!" Éloïse gripped the rail so tight her hands ached.

They couldn't reach it. The rope was too short!

"Throw it again," she pleaded.

One of the figures disappeared beneath a breaker.

"No."

The other sank a moment later, just as the rope splashed the spot where they had been drifting.

"No!" Éloïse ran along the rail, begging the men to resurface. "Luc, where are you?"

She called back to the crew, to Jacques, who held the other end of the rope. "Throw the line again!"

His shoulders sagged, but he did, aiming for the spot Luc had been. The line bobbed in the waves, alone and abandoned.

Éloïse stared at the end, waiting for her husband to reappear and take back command of his ship.

The rain faded to a drizzle.

The wind slowed to a breeze.

The waves calmed.

Still, there was no sign of Éloïse's *destin.*

She gasped as the sun returned, and sank to the side of the rail. Her head fell to her palms as her shoulders quaked. Her warm tears cooled upon reaching her icy hands, the hands Luc would never hold again.

***

Luc was gone. So was Gilbert, and the boy, and Armand. No amount of wishing would bring back the captain of the ship, the one man keeping the rest in line.

Éloïse pulled her blankets tighter around her knees, finding comfort in the security they offered. Having barricaded her door, she hoped the rest of the men wouldn't be able to break through. She heard them whispering late at night.

The widow has been nothing but a curse to our ship. Get rid of her. Quickly. Quietly.

Éloïse shuddered. She stroked Fifi, who lay curled up by her side, and turned back to her books. The one open in her lap held the key, she knew it. It contained so many different ailments and their symptoms. If only her headache would quit throbbing long enough to focus.

Dysentery: Caused by inflamed intestines. Symptoms include diarrhea, constipation, and fever.

No, Éloïse was looking for something that included stomach cramps.

Cholera: Caused by poor fecal cleaning habits. Symptoms include nausea, vomiting, and diarrhea. It is contagious.

That was closer. She rubbed her legs, where what felt like a team of ants were parading up and down her skin.

Hives: Itchy, red splotches on the skin, caused by an allergy.

She pushed down her stockings to check her legs. The only red spots were the lines where her nails had scraped the skin. No bumps or rash, but maybe her heavy eyes were playing tricks on her.

Epilepsy: Characterized by sleep loss, convulsions, and unconsciousness.

She snapped the book closed in frustration. Epilepsy was a disease of the mind, and was usually isolated to one person. How could several crew members all be experiencing its symptoms?

Fifi sat up, his little ears perked forward.

Men were in the corridor just outside.

"…wind is gone again," Alain complained.

"Then we'll have to tell the captain…" Jacques continued, his voice trailing off as they walked on.

Éloïse released her tense hold on her blankets, flexing her sore fingers. Her stomach rumbled, painfully complaining of the lack of a decent meal. She plucked half a roll from her nightstand, having snuck out to the galley the night before. Her thievery was yet another reason to barricade the door.

Munching on the bread speckled with tiny black grains, Éloïse turned back to her book.

St. Anthony's Fire: A common ailment among the poor, this disease is characterized by headaches, stomach discomfort, itching, and hallucinations. Not contagious. Suspected of being caused by bad rye.

That sounded closer, but Luc never sailed with rye on board. He could afford to feed his crew better.

A hundred bugs skittered up Éloïse's toes, legs, and torso, and she screeched.

Her book landed haphazard on the bed as she leaped up, furiously scratching and rubbing the sensation. She pulled at her dress, fully expecting to see huge beetles crawling all over her. Her quick glance at her chest revealed none, but she felt them, she knew they were there. She had to get them off!

"Beetles, beetles everywhere. Scoot, Fifi!"

The cat yowled when Éloïse kicked him away from the bed. The last thing she needed was for all these bugs to jump into his fur.

She fiercely shook her skirts, trying to get rid of the bugs, but nothing fell out. Éloïse ripped the dress over her head and cast it into the mess of an armoire.

Standing in only her shift and stockings, Éloïse finally had to conclude that there were no beetles. Only skin that itched like mad. The sensation was fading now.

Panting, she glanced back to the book and its description of St. Anthony's Fire. Gilbert had talked about the beetles as well. He'd been hallucinating, he'd had the headaches and stomach cramps like everyone else.

And now his body rested at the bottom of the ocean.

A cold shudder rippled through Éloïse as she pictured the black depths, hundreds of kilometers from the surface of the water, sunshine, and life-giving air. She wouldn't succumb. She wouldn't. Luc wanted her to safely make it to New Orleans.

Knock, knock.

"*Madame*, we need to talk."

It was Conrad, the acting captain. Éloïse gasped.

He knocked again. "*Madame*, open up."

"No. Go away, sir!"

"*Madame*, you must listen." Conrad's voice sounded urgent. "The ship is taking on water faster than we can bail it out. Armand has already drowned. The captain demands that we abandon ship."

Éloïse shook her head as she backed against the wall, her chin trembling. She pulled her blanket with her, clutching the woven material as she would a lifeline. "Armand drowned in the storm, and so did Luc. Get away from me, Conrad."

"*Madame!*" Conrad beat rapidly on the door, but the chest blocking it held firm. "Cook, come help me. Jacques, you too."

Gasping, Éloïse watched as the chest bounced bit by bit from the weight of three sailors pushing against the door. She dropped to the floor and threw her blanket over her head.

Pound.

Pound.

"Lord, don't let them break through," she pleaded from her curled-up position in the corner by her bed.

"*Madame.* Éloïse."

She frowned. That voice sounded like Luc.

"Éloïse, where are you? Didn't you hear? We must go."

Éloïse peeked out of her hiding place just as large hands grabbed her under the shoulders.

Panicked, she screamed, but the hands held her tight.

"Éloïse, listen to me," Luc demanded, and his familiar voice made Éloïse pause.

It was a miracle. Somehow, it was indeed her *destin* who stood before her, gripping her arms and now pulling her toward the door.

"A firm hand is all it takes, Captain," Luc said, nodding to Conrad, who stood in the doorway.

Éloïse ground her feet into the floor, and Luc morphed into Cook. She saw every detail of his greasy, scraggly beard now.

"Get your hands off me!" Éloïse fought hard, trying to free herself from his tight grip.

Cook held on all the tighter, and Jacques pinned her arms together.

"Captain says abandon ship, and that's what we do," Cook growled. Conrad watched with a sober, sorrowful gaze. Éloïse was powerless against the men. They dragged her up the stairs and out on deck.

The sun beat down, bright and yellow in the clear blue sky. The ocean was calm. Brown spots of *sargassum* bobbed on the gentle waves.

"The rowboat is over there," Jacques said, nodding to the starboard side. Numbly, Éloïse let them take her.

This all had to be a mistake. Headaches, stomach cramps, and itching. Then hallucinations. Éloïse had seen the signs in the others. She had seen them in herself. She might be seeing another one right now.

"St. Anthony's Fire," she whispered, looking at the ship and sparkling sea in a new light. Her stomach pained her, her head ached, bugs crawled all over her skin, and it all might just be a figment of her imagination. She laughed. "It's St. Anthony's Fire!"

There was rye in the grain stores. Éloïse should've realized what those black specks in the gruel and bread were. The crew just had to stop eating the bread, and everyone would be fine!

"The woman's gone mad," Jacques muttered. "Just like Gilbert and Armand."

"No matter." Cook forced her all the way to the rail. "Captain says abandon ship. Over you go, *Madame*."

Humoring him, Éloïse peeked over the edge. Below, with waves sloshing against its side, was the little rowboat. Masters Antoine and Sebastien were already seated there with the surviving boy and Alain. Master Raoul descended on a rope ladder that Alain held steady.

"Mind your step, sir!" the boy called up, watching Raoul intently.

Éloïse smirked at Jacques. "You really expect me to go down there, even in a dream?"

"This is no dream, *Madame*," Conrad declared. "The *Rosalie* is sinking. We stand a better chance of rowing to New Orleans than remaining here. Captain's orders."

The tight grips on her arms were tangible, as was the solid deck beneath her feet and the humidity from the deep, suffocating water below. Conrad was serious. The realization washed over her as a cold shadow. She tried to flee. "No. I won't go over. There is nothing wrong with the ship!"

Cook slapped her. "*Madame* Blanchard, either you take the ladder willingly, or we toss you down to the boat. I guarantee the latter won't be comfortable."

He meant to toss her overboard. The cruel man meant to break her spine on the side of the rowboat and leave her to drown, unable to save herself.

She tried to break free. "I won't go!"

Fifi meowed behind her, and Éloïse pulled against the men to go to him. They would never force her if she held the good luck charm.

"Fine, you made your choice." Cook grunted. "Jacques, swing her over on three."

Éloïse screeched, dropping herself to the deck like a dead weight and pointing her feet to the rail to use as stoppers.

"One."

The men hoisted her up, lifting her through the air with a whoosh that made her feel like she was flying. Her stomach traveled up to her throat.

"Two."

She pushed her feet against the rail, arching her back. Could she somersault backwards?

"Three."

The men pushed against her back and released her arms. The blue ocean stretched endlessly across the horizon then filled her view as she screamed.

The water came up fast. She had no time to take a breath before her face and body plunged into the waves in a white spray of bubbles.

Don't breathe, don't breathe.

Éloïse's lungs screamed for air. She kicked and clawed the water to reach the surface. She saw the sun just above her head, right next to the shadow that was the ship and rowboat. Hands dipped into the water. Men's voices calling her name sounded muffled to her ears.

"*Ma colombe.*"

Éloïse stopped clawing and turned to Luc's voice, which sounded perfectly clear to her ears.

There he was, just out of reach and as entirely submerged in the water as she was.

He didn't look like he was drowning. He was dressed as she had last seen him, casually attired in his white shirt, trousers, and scuffed blue boots. His brown hair gracefully swirled about his face. His beard was neatly trimmed. His green eyes sparkled as they hadn't since leaving the harbor at Brest. He smiled.

Mon destin.

Luc extended a hand to her. "They won't save you, *ma colombe.*"

Éloïse glanced up to where the hands were still dipped into the salty water. She heard her name once, but it sounded faint and far away. No rope was sent down for her. No respect for decency had been granted her when they had yanked her out of her quarters in her undergarments. No, they wouldn't truly save her.

Éloïse reached for Luc.

***

SHIP DESERTED. — A letter from Nassau, in the Bahamas, bearing date the 27th of August, has the following narrative: — "A singular fact has taken place within the last few days. A large French vessel, bound from Hamburgh to the Havannah, was met by one of our small coasters, and was discovered to be completely abandoned. The greater part of her sails were set, and she did not appear to have sustained any damage. The cargo, composed of wines, fruits, silks, etc., was of very considerable value, and was in a most perfect condition. The captain's papers were all secure in their proper place. The soundings gave three feet of water in the hold, but there was no leak whatever. The only living beings found on board were a cat, some fowls, and several canaries half dead with hunger. The cabins of the officers and passengers were very elegantly furnished, and everything indicated that they had been only recently deserted. In one of them were found several articles belonging to a lady's toilet, together with a quantity of ladies' wearing apparel thrown hastily aside, but not a human being was to be found on board. The vessel, which must have been left within a very few hours, contained several bales of goods addressed to different merchants in Havannah. She is very large, recently built, and called the *Rosalie*. Of her crew no intelligence has been received."

(*Times* (London), November 6, 1840, p. 6, col. 3.)

In Her Reflection

Heather Hayden

Part One: 18 Years Old

She almost had me. Aileen crouched against the side of her bed, the hardwood bed frame pressing into her spine. A throbbing ache in her left foot matched the pain on her right shin. Her breaths came in sharp gasps, tinged cinnamon by the faint traces of toothpaste from brushing her teeth hours ago. Fingers clenched into her arms, Aileen dug her bare toes into the soft carpet, anchoring herself in her room.

Moonlight pouring through the gaps in her window blinds carved sharp shapes from the darkness. Window on the left wall from the door—check. Desk on the right wall, with accompanying chair—check. Bunk beds on the far wall—check.

Mirror hanging to the right of the bedroom door— check. The ancient, iron-rimmed monstrosity glinted in the moonlight that shimmered across its flat surface. Aileen was in the shadows by her bed, but she could see a flicker of brown in the mirror. Brown, like her hair. Brown, like the hair of her doppelganger, the girl in the mirror.

Even that glimpse was enough to freeze the air in Aileen's lungs. She shuddered and huddled closer to her bed. Exhaustion dragged at her eyelids, trying to coax her back under the blankets, but she resisted. Sleeping had gotten her

"

into trouble in the first place. Somehow, Neelia had coaxed her out of bed and across the room.

The Lego set strewn across the floor had saved her. Aileen's foot still throbbed where she had stepped on a particularly pointy piece, but she welcomed the ache. Better that than the alternative.

"Aileen," beckoned the whisper, more an echo than a full sound. It was her own voice, but the one she heard in video recordings, not when she spoke aloud. Neelia's voice. "Aileen."

"Nice try," she retorted under her breath, hugging herself more tightly. Her fingernails dug into her arms, sharp pain grounding her in reality.

"Aileen…"

She shook her head, drawing in deep breaths. Her heart thudded against her ribs. Neelia couldn't do anything to her. Except whisper. And whispering had almost been enough. If she hadn't dumped the box of Legos on the floor before going to bed… A shudder ran down her back. Her spine ached from the pressure of the bed frame, but after the panicked leap across the room to her bed, Aileen couldn't summon the energy to move.

Unwilling to rest, but exhausted from spending the day packing for college, Aileen kept her eyes fixed on her window and the slowly shifting moonlight. She refused to look at the mirror again, to acknowledge the presence of the person…demon…doppelganger who had almost taken her place. Again.

As the adrenaline began to seep from her limbs, leaving them shaking with fatigue, her mind started to drift. Unbidden, memories began to climb out of the black pits where she kept them buried, dragged forward by the deep-seated fear that saturated both this night and those recollections. Aileen welcomed them. They reminded her why she couldn't let her guard down.

Ever.

Part Two: 6…or 7 Years Old?

The first memory to surface was still polished and sharp, rather than dimmed by the years. She'd been six—maybe seven?—and her parents were worried about her obsession with her "imaginary" friend. One night, while sneaking down to the kitchen for a cookie, she overheard them talking and paused just outside the closed kitchen door.

"It's not healthy," Dad snapped in a low whisper. "Most kids her age are making real friends on the playground. Her teacher says she spends recess sitting in the corner, watching the other kids. When Mrs. Mottle asks her if she wants to play with them, Aileen just says they aren't as fun as Neelia."

Mom and Dad had insisted that using "Aileen" for both of them was confusing, so Aileen had scrawled her name backward to spell a new one for Neelia. Neelia liked the idea. After all, they were mirror images of each other, right down to the crescent moon birthmark on Aileen's left shin that matched the one on Neelia's right shin.

A sigh from Mom stopped Aileen's hand reaching for the kitchen door's handle. Her stomach rumbled, but her parents' tones sent a feeling like a bellyache through her midsection. Maybe she didn't deserve a cookie.

"It's perfectly healthy for a little girl to have an imaginary friend," Mom said, her words punctuated with a quiet slurp. She was probably drinking beer. Beer tended to make Mom angry and loud, so Aileen took a step backward. She could always come back for a cookie later.

The floor creaked underfoot, but Dad's voice covered the sound.

"She's too old for this imaginary friend business. Jerry gave me the number for a therapist. Maybe we should take her over there this week—"

"No!"

Aileen crept back up the stairs. Her heart hurt, like it did when she spilled grape juice on the living room carpet and Mom got mad. Somehow, her parents were angry because of her. Were they mad they couldn't see Neelia? It wasn't her fault; she'd tried and tried to get them to see her friend.

Aileen took the last few stairs as fast as her legs could churn and dashed down to her bedroom.

Neelia jumped forward as Aileen approached the giant mirror hanging on the wall. Not too close, because Mom and Dad had forbidden Aileen from touching it—it was old and she might damage it. Her grandmother, Mom's mom, had left it to baby Aileen in her will. Aileen loved it, not for its worn, gilded edges or smooth silver surface, but for the friend it held inside.

"No cookies?" Neelia's face fell, a reflection of Aileen's disappointment. She loved when Aileen sneaked cookies upstairs, because it meant she could eat them too.

Aileen shook her head. Her eyes pinched against the sting of tears. "Mommy and Daddy are mad at me."

Neelia frowned. "Why?" The brown-haired girl sat down, cross-legged, on the carpet.

Aileen sat as well and cradled her chin in her palms. "They don't believe you exist."

"They can't see me." Neelia pouted, her bottom lip quivering. "It's not fair."

This was true. No matter how many times they had tried to show her parents that Neelia was there, all they saw was Aileen's reflection.

Neelia pressed her hand against the mirror, her pout vanishing into a bright smile. "Do you want to play?"

Aileen shook her head, shoulders slumped. She'd really wanted the cookie.

"Come play with me," Neelia begged, resting her forehead against the mirror next to her hand. "I'm bored."

Releasing a long sigh, like Mom had, Aileen stood and walked over to the mirror. "Don't feel like it."

"But you were gone all day." Neelia started to cry. "You always go off to school and leave me here with nothing to do and I miss you and it isn't fair."

Not fair was something Aileen understood, and she felt bad for making Neelia cry. "Okay," she said, reaching out a hand. "I'll play with you."

She'd misjudged her distance from the mirror, however, and her hand touched the surface. For a brief second, panic welled within her—Mom and Dad would be *really* mad if she broke it—but a strange pressure squeezed her from all sides, and everything went dark for a moment.

Then she was standing in her room again, except it looked odd. Aileen looked around, frowning. Something was wrong, but she couldn't quite tell what.

"Aileen, it's time for bed." Mom's voice brought her head toward the bedroom door, but it remained shut, even though the hinges were creaking.

"Yes, Mommy," came her voice, except it wasn't her voice. It was Neelia's voice.

Aileen looked at the mirror and saw Mom tucking Neelia into her bed. Something pressed against her throat. Her mouth opened and released a scream.

Mom didn't seem to notice. She kissed Neelia's forehead, patted the blankets, and then left, turning out the light. The room was dark after that, and Aileen screamed again.

"Shhh! You're hurting my ears." Neelia's whisper came from nearby. Aileen squinted and finally began to make out the faint shape of her double standing in the middle of her bedroom.

"What's going on?" Aileen started to cry. "I want Mommy!"

"I want Mommy too." Neelia sounded close to tears herself. "It's not fair you always get to be tucked in."

Aileen coughed, choking on a sob. "You get tucked in every night, too." She knew Neelia did, she saw Mom's reflection tucking in Neelia in the mirror.

Neelia shook her head. "It's not real. It isn't. It never is. I never feel anything. Not like you."

Aileen pressed against the surface of the mirror, but it was as solid and unyielding as stone. "I'm sorry. Please let me out."

Neelia hesitated. "I don't want to go back in."

"Please!" Aileen begged.

"Tomorrow," Neelia offered. "But you have to let me be tucked in and go to school sometimes."

Aileen nodded. "I promise, I promise!"

Neelia turned away and went back to bed.

The next morning, Aileen watched as Neelia got dressed and headed downstairs for breakfast. Hours passed in a silent drone of boredom. Then Neelia returned, as cheerful as Aileen usually was.

"No one realized it was me instead of you," Neelia said. "We played tag at recess! It was fun."

Aileen had never played tag. She stared out the mirror at Neelia and wished she was standing in her own room. "Switch with me now."

"Not yet!" Neelia grabbed a bunch of dolls and plastic horses. "Play with me first!"

It was strange to pick up the reflections of her toys, to see them in her hand without feeling their hard plastic or soft plush surfaces. But Aileen did her best. Was this how Neelia spent her time in the mirror? Aileen's chest hurt thinking about it, but it hurt even more watching Mom read a chapter of their bedtime story about a girl and her dragon to Neelia.

When the chapter was finished, Mom kissed Neelia good night and turned off the light as she closed the door.

"Neelia," Aileen whispered, her heart sinking into her chest. "Neelia, where are you?"

Her doppelganger was a faint image in the mirror that let Aileen view her room. "You promise we can switch again?"

Aileen nodded. "Yes!"

Their hands touched the mirror's surface in unison, and an odd stretching sensation pulled her body until she thought she might fly apart like her doll Sally did when Aileen tugged Sally's head off. But the feeling was a feeling, and after nothing for a day, she welcomed it.

Her toes burrowed into the soft carpet under her feet, and she hugged her arms against herself, feeling the warm flannel of her favorite pajamas. Memories jostled in her mind; she could *remember* going to school today, the feeling of running across the playground, laughing with the other kids. It made her gasp.

"It's like I was there!"

Neelia nodded. "I could remember people's names and stuff." She sniffled and looked around the room within the mirror. "I hate it in here."

Aileen did too.

But a promise was a promise, and she kept it. They took turns at random, though Neelia never stayed out for more than a day. With Neelia's help, Aileen made friends at school, though she still preferred spending time with her reflection and her schoolbooks. Her parents sent her to a therapist briefly, but Aileen's insistence that her imaginary friend no longer existed soon got her out of those visits.

The arrangement worked well. For a time.

Part Three: 10 Years Old

Two days after Aileen turned ten, her parents had planned a trip to Grandma's. They were going to help pack up everything in the farmhouse she lived in. Dad had decided his mother should move to a place closer by, an assisted living home, because her memory was starting to fail.

"I wish I was going with you."

Aileen looked up from packing her red suitcase, the one Neelia had convinced Mom to buy a few days ago. "There's no way we could transport the mirror. It might break." She chewed her lip. "It's only for a week. I've been gone that long before."

"It's so boring." Neelia groaned and flopped face down. Despite the position, her voice still came clearly from the mirror. "You better bring back something cool for me."

"We're just visiting Grandma to help her get everything packed up." Aileen smiled. "Maybe I can ask her for one of her photo albums. She probably won't want all of them."

"Boring," Neelia repeated.

Aileen shrugged. She loved her grandmother's photographs. A hobbyist photographer, Grandma's house was filled with albums stacked on bookcases and frames hanging on walls. "I'll try to find something interesting for you."

"Aileen!" Mom called from downstairs. "Hurry up! It's time to go!"

"Coming!" Aileen shoved her hairbrush into her bulging suitcase and zipped it up. With a grunt, she hefted it from the bed onto the floor. "I'll see you next Saturday, Neelia."

"Urgh." Neelia lifted her head a fraction off the floor, still scowling. "Have fun." Her tone told Aileen she only half-meant it.

"I will!" Aileen grinned as she lugged her suitcase down the stairs. She loved visiting Grandma. Neelia would too, if she ever did—though Aileen couldn't imagine letting her reflection go in her place.

Three hours later, Grandma enveloped Aileen in a cloud of lilac perfume, smothering her with kisses and hugs.

"You're already so grown up! My little granddaughter... I remember when you were just a babe in my arms."

Aileen smiled up at her grandmother as Mom and Dad carried luggage into the house. "You remember me?"

More wrinkles appeared on Grandma's forehead as she raised her eyebrows. "Of course I do! How could I forget my own granddaughter?"

Dad shook his head at Aileen from the hallway, but she just smiled smugly back. He was wrong. Grandma would never forget who she was. Especially not once she moved to their town.

"Would you like to see my latest pictures?" Grandma asked, taking Aileen's hand and leading her into the house. "I saw some deer in the backyard last week. Just got the photos back; such a dear boy, little Jerry Hunt, driving all the way here and back again with my film. There were two does and a buck. No, just three does, I think. Or was there a buck as well?" She paused and looked down at the worn carpet in the hallway, her pale blue eyes absently tracing the swooping design.

Aileen tugged on Grandma's hand. "I want to see the pictures!"

"What pictures, dear?" Her grandmother frowned. "I haven't had any developed since I saw the deer last week."

That silenced Aileen for a brief moment. Grandma had forgotten the first half of their conversation so quickly. That never used to happen. Stomach twisting, Aileen squeezed her grandmother's hand. She wouldn't let Grandma forget her.

"Is something wrong, dear?" Grandma's eyebrows knit together like the cable stitch of her sweater.

Aileen shook her head and forced a smile. "I haven't seen those pictures yet."

"Let's go take a look, shall we? And maybe some of your baby pictures, too."

Aileen rolled her eyes. "Those are boring." Which reminded her. "Could I take some pictures home with me?"

Grandma released a sigh and brushed her hand over the frame of a picture hanging on the wall. The picture was faded but still showed a young couple sitting on a porch swing, arms wrapped around each other. "I wish John were here. I wouldn't need to move if he was."

Unsure what to say, Aileen coaxed her grandmother down the hall to the library, where most of the photo albums were kept.

A week later, Aileen came home with an armload of pictures to hang on her wall.

"Boring," Neelia commented, and she proceeded to ask question after question as Aileen found a place for each picture in her room.

"Did she remember you?"

"Of course she did!" Aileen hit the hanging nail a little harder than necessary with the hammer.

"Did she ask about me?"

"No. She hasn't in ages." No one did anymore. Aileen had stopped talking about her reflection ages ago.

"I guess she forgot me." Neelia's shoulders slumped. "Will you forget about me someday, too?"

"I don't know. I hope not." The thought was unsettling; Neelia was Aileen's best friend. What would life be like without her?

"Will you keep the mirror with you?" Neelia pressed her hand against the glass. "Even if you move someday?"

Aileen nodded as she adjusted the picture she had just hung so that it was straight. "And I'll pack it in lots of bubblewrap so that it doesn't break."

Neelia shuddered. "That's a good idea." A smile spread across her face. "Did you get any bubblewrap?"

In response, Aileen unzipped the outer pocket of her suitcase and pulled out a bundle of scraps she'd collected from wrapping pictures with Grandma. "Loads."

"Yay!" Neelia bounced up and down. "I'm going to pop so many! Let me out, let me out!"

Aileen laughed. "Okay, but only for a bit. I need to hang the other pictures."

For a moment, she stood in front of the mirror, staring at her reflection. She hated this part.

"Come on," Neelia urged. "It's been forever."

"I know." Aileen took a deep breath, pressed her hand against the mirror, and closed her eyes.

The mirror-world pressed in around her, choking in its absence of any sense of touch. She shivered, without feeling the sensation of shivering, and watched as Neelia popped bubble after bubble. Each sharp snap made her jump a little from shock. Neelia had told her once that coming out of the mirror felt like popping a bubble. The comparison had stuck in Aileen's mind. She laughed along with her reflection, but she couldn't wait to pop back out.

She hated the mirror.

Part Four: 14 Years Old

Aileen was fourteen when her grandmother passed away. For a few years, Grandma had lived at the nearby nursing home. Near the end, she barely recognized her son, much less her granddaughter, as she drifted in and out of reality.

The day Grandma left the world, Dad came home late. The nursing home had insisted he stop by to pick up his mother's belongings.

Aileen was curled up on the living room couch, surrounded by a sea of tissues. She had found his voicemail on her phone after charging it when she got home. She'd been crying since then. She hadn't even gone upstairs to tell Neelia yet. Dad set down a cardboard box and settled on the couch next to Aileen, opening his arms. She buried her face in his chest and sobbed. His hand gently rubbed her back as he cried too.

"I have something here for you," Dad said, finally pulling away and reaching for the cardboard box. He opened it and pulled out a thick leather photo album. "She wanted me to give you this. Said she loved looking at the pictures with you."

Aileen clasped the familiar album to her chest, still sniffling. Dad patted her back.

"Why don't you take a look at it? I need to fix supper. Your mother is coming home late."

"Okay." Box of tissues tucked under her arm, Aileen went upstairs.

"What happened?" Neelia asked as Aileen entered the bedroom.

"Grandma died." Aileen wiped her nose with a tissue. "I'm going to look at the photo album she left me."

The doppelganger offered a sympathetic look. "I'm so sorry, Aileen."

Aileen looked away from the mirror, tears welling in her eyes again. Neelia didn't know Grandma like Aileen did. She hadn't been crying for the past two hours—didn't even have the red nose or puffy eyes of someone who had. Another time, Aileen might have been jealous of her doppelganger's perfection. Right now, all she felt was a deep ache in her chest, like someone had carved everything out.

She closed her door and crossed her room to her bed. "I just want to be alone for a while."

Neelia's voice rose a fraction. "But I want to see the photos too! Please, Aileen?"

"Not right now." Aileen grasped the canopy's curtain and drew it across, ignoring Neelia's pleading. She was glad Mom had agreed to a canopy bed. Mom had seen it as her daughter finally showing interest in "girly" things. Aileen appreciated the privacy it offered.

She turned on the tiny bedlamp that sat on her nightstand and snuggled her back into a pile of pillows. The photo album rested on her knees, heavy and solid and carrying a slight whiff of lilacs—Grandma's favorite perfume.

Aileen blinked back tears and opened the cover. Her fingers traced the edges of the old instant photos. Some of them were well-worn; others crisper in colors and detail. The thick paper pages crackled as she flipped slowly through the album. The photos were in no specific order, unsurprisingly—it reminded her a lot of Grandma's memories, in a way. All scattered about and mixed together in unexpected ways.

Here was her dad as a kid, riding on a tricycle. The next photo was one of him at graduation—high school, she thought. And the next was another baby. The photo was unlabeled. Aileen pulled it out of its slot and flipped it over. No date or name.

With careful fingers, she tucked it back into its place then traced a finger over the waving hands and feet. The picture had been captured as a candid—slightly blurry but still sharp enough to make out the baby's bright eyes and a small mark on the left shin. Frowning, Aileen looked a little closer. The mark was shaped like a lopsided crescent moon.

"It's me!" She grinned. Her baby self looked so silly, lying on her back in a diaper. So innocent. The grin faded a bit. Back then, she hadn't known Neelia. At least, not as far as she could remember, not that she remembered being that young. Had Neelia even been around then? It was strange imagining her doppelganger as a baby, but then, Neelia must have come from somewhere.

Aileen's finger traced over the mark again. She still had that birthmark, though it was smaller than it looked in the photograph. Most people didn't even see it, especially after she put on a summer tan. You had to look really closely—

Aileen's finger froze on top of the mark. She looked from the picture down to her legs sticking out from her shorts. Her left leg was half tucked up under her right in such a way that she could see the mark on the inner side of her shin. Her *left* leg.

The leg in the photograph, on the left, where the mark was, was actually the baby's *right* leg.

Aileen sucked in a deep breath and slipped the photograph out again. She handled it gingerly, as if she expected it to burst into flames. After setting it on the bed beside her, she flipped through more pages, seeking every baby picture she could find. Some were of her father, or uncle, or her two aunts. But a few were of her, and she plucked each from its tabs.

Spreading all of the pictures across her blanket, Aileen arranged them by age as best she could—only a couple had dates. Some showed enough growth to be discernable. Many had her wrapped in a blanket or dressed in various cute outfits, but a few showed her legs.

Except for the first one she had found, all of the images—some of her as a young baby, others of her as she approached toddler size—had the birthmark on the baby's left leg. The quality of pictures also shifted. The first one had a graininess to it that a couple others shared, but later ones were sharper, as though the photographer had gotten better at focusing or switched cameras.

A block of ice settled in Aileen's chest, and she swept all of the photos but one into a pile with shaking fingers.

She was Aileen. Not Neelia. Neelia was a ghost, a shadow, a reflection that lived only in the mirror. Something that was half-friend and half-specter. Something that would be altogether dangerous if she ever saw that photo and realized what it meant.

Aileen slipped the pile of photos into the front of the album and set it aside. One photo still lay on her bedspread.

A smiling, bright-eyed baby stared accusingly at Aileen, the wrong-sided birthmark like a bloodstain on her leg.

Aileen slipped it into her pocket and went downstairs to hide it in her coat. Then she went through every other photo album they owned. She couldn't find another picture with the flipped birthmark. But that didn't mean one didn't exist. Grandma had taken thousands of photos of Aileen since she was born.

Not that it mattered if a picture existed or not. The moment she swapped places with Neelia, her reflection would have the ability to recall Aileen's memory of seeing the picture. And there was only one solution to that, a solution Aileen couldn't bear to consider.

For the next few days, Aileen huddled in misery in her bed, terrified that Neelia would ask to come out. Neelia did not, perhaps out of respect for Aileen's grief. But if she knew the truth… Aileen shook her head, tears slipping down her face. Neelia could never learn the truth. Would never learn the truth. If she did, she might never let Aileen out of the mirror again.

That Saturday was cold and cloudy with a looming threat of rain. The burial ceremony was short, with Dad giving a eulogy that made Aileen and her mother and all of Grandma's family and friends cry. Before the coffin was lowered, everyone lined up to say good-bye one last time.

Aileen slipped the picture under Grandma's hand and whispered, "I love you."

When Mom later asked what the picture had been of, Aileen said, "It was a cute baby picture I found in her photo album. I thought she'd like to have it with her."

Dad got teary-eyed, Mom sniffled, and Aileen stared out the car window at the shrinking cemetery gate as rain streaked down to paint everything gray.

She knew what she had to do. Aileen could never trust that Neelia wouldn't discover the truth. Leaning her forehead against the chilly car window, Aileen blinked back tears. Her reflection did the same; Neelia only existed in Grandma's mirror. This reflection, blurred by tears and water running down the outside, was nothing more than a shadow of Aileen's pain.

"I wish I'd never gotten that stupid mirror," she whispered to herself.

When she got home, Aileen went upstairs and broke the news.

"I can't switch places with you anymore."

Neelia's jaw dropped, her eyes widening with shock. "What do you mean, you can't? Aileen, you promised!"

"I know I did. But I can't now. I'm sorry." Aileen leaned against her bed and pressed her palms against her eyes. "If you want, I'll ask Mom and Dad to get rid of the mirror. Maybe you can find someone else."

"You're joking." Desperation threaded through Neelia's voice like sharp needles. "You can't be serious, Aileen. You're just upset right now. Grief, right? You can't leave me in here forever. You promised you'd take turns with me. You promised!"

"I hate it in there!" Aileen sucked in a breath, lowering her voice. She didn't need her parents walking in because she was yelling. "I've always hated it in there. I don't want to switch anymore, Neelia. I'm sorry. But I won't."

"Please," Neelia begged, folding her hands against her chest. "I hate it in here too, Aileen. We're friends… Aren't we friends? Please don't do this."

Aileen slid up and back onto her bed and grabbed the corner of the curtain. "I'm sorry." She yanked the curtain down.

Neelia's sobs filled the room, echoed by Aileen's own tears.

It's for the best, Aileen told herself. But it was hard to believe that. Her chest ached, as though someone had punched a hole into it. No, two holes. She'd just lost her grandmother, and now she feared she'd lost her best friend.

But what choice did she have?

Part Five: 18 Years Old, Redux

"Aileen," Neelia whispered. "Aileen…"

Shaking herself out of the iron grip of her memories, Aileen looked up at the mirror's faint outline. A smile slowly spread across her face, chasing away the terror she had felt. Standing, she moved across the room to the light switch and flipped it on.

Her eyes took a moment to adjust to the flood of light. Neelia stood in the mirror, Aileen's mirror image in every way, from her short-cropped hair to her sleep-wrinkled shorts.

"Aileen!" Neelia smiled back. "You're leaving tomorrow for college. Don't you want to talk to me before you go?" She showed no hint of animosity, but Aileen wasn't fooled. After she'd refused to switch places again, Neelia had freaked out. Yelled. Screamed. Pleaded. Aileen had stood firm, even threatened to have her parents remove the mirror, though part of her didn't want to lose her closest friend. The one she had told all of her dreams, her crushes, her secrets.

Well, all of her secrets…save one.

Neelia had chosen to stay, and even became amicable again. Their friendship had recovered. There had been times when Aileen had been almost tempted to let Neelia out again. Each time, she had resisted. No matter how buried her memories might be, there was always a chance her reflection would discover them.

"What do you want to talk about?" Aileen asked, curling her fingers into fists. "The fact you were trying to force me to switch?"

Neelia folded her arms. "I thought you might listen to reason if I could get you in here again. Remind you of how awful it is."

"I remember." Aileen shuddered. "I hated it in here."

"I hate it every single day." Neelia gestured toward the Legos on the floor. "I wondered why you did that. How'd you know?"

"I had a bruise on my leg this morning." Aileen prodded her right shin, wincing at the pain.

Neelia scowled. "Serves you right. You fell out of bed and landed on the suitcase I told you not to leave by the bed."

"You weren't concerned about me," Aileen snapped. "You just wanted a clear path to the mirror so you could lure me in!"

"I wasn't trying to lure you. I just wanted to switch so we could talk."

"Talk about what?"

"Bringing the mirror to college with you. I don't want to stay here, it's going to be so boring." Neelia's voice broke. "Please don't leave me behind."

"So you can have another chance to force me to let you pop out?" Aileen released a bark of laughter. "Not a chance."

"It was just a bit of fun." Neelia pouted. "You're a remarkably deep sleeper. Last night was the first time it almost worked. Would have, except for that stupid suitcase."

"You've tried it before?" Aileen's heart skipped a few beats at the thought. She could have woken up in the mirror, never to escape again, if Neelia had managed the switch.

"Not much else to do in here, is there? It's been four years, Aileen. You *promised* you'd share with me. It's not fair. Take the mirror with you!"

Another time, she might have been tempted. Aileen closed her eyes, remembering all the good times they'd had together. All the memories they'd shared. But there was one particular memory that overshadowed all of them. The truth.

"I'm sorry." She opened her eyes but couldn't bring herself to meet Neelia's pleading gaze. "The mirror's being moved to the new house. Mom and Dad will probably put it in a guest room."

"Ugh." Neelia slumped against the surface of the mirror. "Come on, Aileen. You can't seriously want to leave me behind. Aren't we friends?"

Aileen moved across the room to stand by her desk. There was a paperweight sitting beside the lamp, neither of which she was bringing with her to college. The paperweight had a flower imbedded in it, a present from a friend years ago. The glass felt heavy, solid in Aileen's grip.

Neelia is never going to give up. If I don't do something, she might actually succeed someday. I can't let that happen. This is my life, not hers.

Aileen's fingers tightened around the paperweight.

"What are you doing?" Neelia's face grew pale as Aileen stalked toward the mirror.

"I wasn't very specific," Aileen said, raising the paperweight. Some small part of her resisted the idea that was forming as she spoke the words. She ignored it. "The *mirror* will be going to the other house, but not all of it. Only the frame. That is, if Mom and Dad feel like salvaging a broken mirror."

"You can't break this," Neelia protested, her voice shaking as she clasped her hands together over her heart. "That's murder."

Aileen gritted her teeth. She'd had the same thought many times in the past few years. What was Neelia, after all? No one else could see her, but when she was outside the mirror, she was as real as Aileen.

Sensing her hesitation, Neelia forced a chuckle. "Besides, breaking a mirror is seven years' bad luck, remember?"

And how many years would Aileen spend in the mirror, should Neelia ever learn the truth?

Her resolve hardened into the rock-hard shape of a paperweight.

"I'll take my chances." Aileen hefted the paperweight, preparing to throw it. The sudden euphoria she felt, knowing that she would soon be free of her reflection, free of the fear that had frozen her in place earlier that night, loosened her tongue. "I don't know how it happened, and I don't care, but I think I'm plenty lucky. After all, I managed to switch places with you when we were just babies."

"What—" Neelia's stricken face shattered into a million screaming reflections.

Aileen held her breath, waiting.

Her doppelganger flickered then disappeared, leaving only Aileen's smirking expression behind.

"I should have done that years ago." Aileen stared at the shards of glass littering the floor beneath the broken mirror. "Goodbye, Neelia. Or should that be Aileen?" After heaving the mirror off its hook and leaning it against the wall, she turned off her light and returned to bed. Her foot still ached, but she rubbed it with the other one until it stopped, then drifted off to sleep.

Later that morning, she carried the last of her things down from her room. "Mom? Dad?"

"Good morning, sweetheart," Mom called from the kitchen. "I'm making pancakes!"

Aileen walked in. "Yum! Um..." She took a deep breath, knowing her mother was going to be upset. "I'm really sorry, Mom, but I accidentally broke the mirror."

"What?" The spatula clattered as it hit the floor. Mom pressed a palm to her left temple, eyes squeezed shut. Her words were clipped short, spit out before emotion could reach them. "Mother's mirror? What happened?"

"It was heavier than I expected and it slipped." Aileen hung her head, playing the part of being upset even though she was still elated that Neelia was no longer a threat. "I'm really, really sorry. I have some money left from this summer—I can pay to have the glass replaced."

A muscle spasmed on Mom's jaw, and then she released a heavy sigh, opened her eyes, and bent down to gather the spatula. Tossing it in the sink, she opened the drawer by the stove and drew out a clean spatula. The new one scraped against the pan as Mom shoved it under each round pancake to flip it. Batter sizzled as it hit the hot pan.

"Mom?" Aileen braced herself for an explosion. Despite the years of therapy, Mom still lost her temper at times.

Another deep sigh. "It's fine, Aileen. Eat your pancakes."

Relieved, Aileen took a seat at the table and dug in. A quiet sniffle brought her head up. She glanced at Mom, still standing at the stove, spatula hanging loosely in her fingers. A single, silent tear slipped down her mother's cheek. That alone almost made Aileen feel guilty about what she had done.

Almost.

After breakfast, Aileen helped Dad load the car.

"Are you excited for college?" Dad asked, slinging the last few bags into the car's trunk. The late August heat plastered what little hair he had left to his scalp.

"Yep." Aileen adjusted the strap of her backpack on her shoulder. Out here, in the bright sun, the pounding heat, it was hard to remember the icy chill that had numbed her bones last night. She smiled and bounced on her toes, feeling for a moment like a little girl again, off on a great adventure. "Thanks for driving me, Dad."

"No problem, kiddo." He wiped his brow on his forearm and raised a hand to the trunk lid. "Is that everything?"

Aileen fanned her face with the packing list. The brief breeze it created against her sweaty skin felt nice. She looked over the list and the pile of belongings stashed in the spacious trunk then nodded. "We're good to go."

"Great."

Mom descended from the house in tears and wrapped Aileen in a tight hug. "I wish I could go with you! Do you have your wallet? Your toothbrush? Enough clothes? The books we got?"

"Yes," Aileen replied, patting Mom's back as she rolled her eyes at Dad. "I'm all set. Good luck with the big showing tomorrow."

Mom sniffed and nodded. "Call us every day so we know how things are going, okay?"

"She can call us on the weekends, dear." Dad rubbed Mom's back. "Every bird has to fly the nest someday."

"Send me pictures of the new place," Aileen added, grinning. "I've only seen the realtor pics so far."

After several more hugs and many more tears, Aileen managed to work her way into the front passenger's seat. Dad spoke with Mom for a few more minutes then slid behind the wheel.

The engine purred to life.

"Road trip time!" Dad punched the stereo button as his phone synced up, and music started to play over the car speakers.

Aileen grinned as she watched the house shrink away as the car headed down the street. Mom waved for a while before she went inside. Aileen waved back. And kept waving, even after Mom vanished from sight. There was someone else to wave goodbye to, after all.

Aileen waved goodbye to the reflection she could no longer see. Who she would never see again. The Aileen whose life she had stolen all those years ago.

Smiling, she turned in her seat and stretched. Five hours until they reached the campus. She couldn't wait to meet her roommate. She and Leah had been messaging back and forth for a couple weeks.

As Dad pulled out onto the interstate, Aileen rolled down the window to enjoy the breeze. A flicker caught her eye in the mirror. Her heart skipped a beat, but a closer look revealed a convertible speeding up behind them. Not Neelia. Of course it wasn't. Neelia was gone.

She laughed and turned the radio up a bit higher so she could hear it over the wind. The convertible zipped by, Dad grumbled about stupid speeders, and Aileen used her door's mirror to check her makeup.

After a fresh coat of lipstick, she winked at herself, pleased with the result.

Her reflection winked back.

your love

Don't Offend a Girl in Love

Cassandra Lee Yieng

As the junior editor of *Mathematical Olympiad Quarterly*, I look forward to the publication of each issue. I focus on my work so intently that I often forget to shave. At least I remember to clean my glasses from time to time so that my eyes don't feel strained.

Damien, the senior editor, was promoted to assistant professorship in June. He's so swamped with work now that he's left me, a final-year MIT math undergraduate, in charge of the MOQ editors' email account. MOQ is based in Hong Kong, but I can work remotely from Cambridge, Massachusetts, during term time. Now it's summer vacation, and I'm back home.

Being pressed for time gives me the "misfortune" of rejecting many articles, but I want it to stay that way. I prefer penning MOQ's articles from scratch with the perk of keeping the glory of publication to myself. After all, I have my own Wikipedia article, and I have spoken at TED and TEDx several times. I'm far better qualified than many others vying for a spot in MOQ.

Damien told me that the quality of MOQ depends on its writers, and he challenged me to delegate my writing as much as possible. "After all," he said, "isn't 'division of labor' the key economic idea behind the Industrial Revolution?"

Reluctantly, I nodded. The truth is, I care too much about this publication to delegate my ideas to other writers. But because Damien requested it, I'm going to give it a try. Provided, of course, I find someone whose writing is as good as mine.

***

July in Hong Kong sucks. The heat and humidity outdoors are a great reason for staying in my air-conditioned study, where I can gaze upon my trophies, certificates, and newspaper clippings detailing the Legend of Prosper Ng (that's me): coming from a little-known high school, this contest-winning schoolboy became a top student aiming for a coveted PhD degree in economics. I can also log on to Facebook and scroll through my list of 4,000+ friends, many of whom are political or academic giants.

I check the MOQ inbox on my laptop at 10 AM and 10 PM sharp because that account is always flooded. It's easier than having to scroll through all of them on my smartphone throughout the day.

This morning, the inbox has 44 unread messages. Most of the emails are submissions; they are automatically acknowledged.

I click on the first non-submission email I come across. It reads:

Tuesday, July 25, 2017 09:34 AM
On MOQ Articles

Dear Prof. Fu and Mr. Ng,

I'm a private Mathematics and French teacher in the Congo. I've been reading MOQ for a while now, and I admire the standard of articles in it. May I ask who may submit to the magazine?

Regards,
Wanda Norton

My first thought: Oh, how I love French—silly me. I grin sheepishly. Remembering Damien's admonition to delegate, I reply:

Tuesday, July 25, 2017 10:05 AM

Dear Ms. Norton,

Thank you very much for your encouragement and inquiry. We are pleased to learn of your interest in MOQ. Anybody may submit articles to MOQ for our consideration and processing. Guidelines for submission can be found on the left side of the contents page of any issue of MOQ.

Best regards,
Prosper Ng

I check the rest of my emails, but before I reach the end of the "unread" deluge, Wanda writes back:

Tuesday, July 25, 2017 10:11 AM

How frequently is the magazine published, and what topics are being planned for the upcoming issue(s)?

Our first three issues were published in January, April, and June respectively, so the publication times are quite irregular for a so-called quarterly. It seems that Wanda is trying her best to meet our expectations. I smirk. This is going to save me a lot of time.

I reply:

Tuesday, July 25, 2017 10:20 AM

MOQ is the flagship newsletter of the Pan-Pacific Mathematical Olympiad (PPMO) to be held in July 2018. We plan to have eight issues of MOQ, and they are being published in this period leading up to the PPMO. As three issues have been published so far, around five issues will be published in the upcoming academic year.

We welcome submission of articles on any topic pertaining to mathematics and/or the mathematical olympiad. To understand the complexity required of your submission(s) in terms of content, please refer to past issues of MOQ here: www.moq.org.hk/issues

As I go to close the mail application, Wanda writes back again. I'm excited rather than annoyed—she seems eager and friendly. If her articles are any good, she'll be the perfect delegate to get Damien off my back.

Tuesday, July 25, 2017 10:23 AM

I would like to submit to MOQ, but I'm having some difficulty finding a good topic to write about, as I have not joined any math olympiad or taught olympiad-level mathematics. What topics might your team suggest I could try writing about? Thank you very much.

Okay, so Wanda wants to write an article for MOQ and doesn't have the foggiest idea on how to begin. I try to suppress the nagging irritation in my chest so that I can respond tactfully.

I tap my pen against my desk, thinking. What would be a good topic for her to write on? What does the magazine need more of? What topics would have the best chances of being accepted by MOQ?

I look at the website I sent Wanda—and I stare at the three kaleidoscopic cover images of MOQ's published issues. MOQ's graphic designers, Joyce and Betty, are both math undergraduates at the Hong Kong University of

Science and Technology. Joyce is a Photoshop maestro, while Betty has won art competitions across Asia. Plus, we haven't had any articles on math and art so far.

That's it! I bang my desk excitedly and reply:

Tuesday, July 25, 2017 10:30 AM

How about writing about the relationship between math and art? There are many possibilities in this area to choose from, e.g., the relationship between math and painting, music, literature, architecture, and dance.

You are free to choose any topic for your article, and we will review it upon your submission. The topic does not have to be specifically about the math olympiad. Any topic about math that suits the level of our readers, who are high school students from around the world, could be worth considering.

***

When I check my email again tonight, Wanda has responded. I'm surprised at her speed.

Tuesday, July 25, 2017 8:01 PM

I propose exploring the works of M. C. Escher, an artist who uses many kinds of tessellation patterns. What do you think?

By accelerating her writing process, I'll be able to report back to Damien with a success story in delegation. He'll be happy to hear that. So I reply:

Tuesday, July 25, 2017 10:29 PM

This sounds like an interesting idea. One possible route is to first discuss tessellation by congruent regular polygons (proving that only three kinds of regular polygons work), then go on to more irregular and complex varieties, such as those of Escher.

We will be happy to review a submission on this topic or any other topic related to math and/ or the math olympiad.

Thanks again for your interest!

As soon as I hit "Send", a gray dialog box displaying a pair of kissing lips fills my screen. Is this a joke or a virus? What in the world is this? I try clicking out of it. The lips continue to pucker disgustingly. I click again. No response. Click. Still there. Click, click, click…click. Those lips are still there.

My cursor turns into a spinning wheel. Every time my computer freezes, it's frustrating. The fan inside the computer whirs loudly, like it's going to explode anytime. I swipe the mousepad frantically, but I can't move my cursor. I bang the keys, trying to break the monitor out of its frozen trance, but I fail.

This is not something I expect before bed. I hold down the power button, and the screen turns to black. The fan goes silent. I go to bed, scowling.

The next morning, the sunlight glares into my eyes. I cover my eyes, yawn, and sneak on my glasses. I trudge to my desk and log in to my laptop. That pesky dialog box is gone, and so is the spinning cursor. My computer works just fine. Phew.

***

I'm back on MIT's campus, where the weather is cooler, the air is fresh, and the sunlight doesn't pry my eyes open. Outside my dorm window, the leaves are turning amber. I missed this campus during the summer. It feels great to be back, despite the constant pile of schoolwork waiting for me.

Damien's busy, too. With too many papers to publish and too little time, he's left me completely in charge of the MOQ account.

It's 10 AM again. Time to check emails. The latest submission is by a Ms. Alyson Cheung, who's reached out to us before. She writes well, but we eventually rejected her articles because her sense of humor was too dark.

Tuesday, August 15, 2017 04:44 AM
Submission to MOQ

Dear Mr. Ng,

I saw that you viewed my profile on LinkedIn. In fact, I also read your public posts on Facebook. On a more personal note, shall we exchange our contact information?

I am submitting the attached article of math and art for the next issue of MOQ. Thank you for your kind consideration, and I am anticipating a swift and favorable reply.

Kind regards,
Alyson Cheung

My first thought: an article on math and art? Is the universe kidding me? I only flirted with the idea a few weeks ago.

Second thought: well, I did recently come across Alyson's LinkedIn profile for the first time, because Joyce and Betty know her—I clicked on her profile out of curiosity.

So I open a new window and visit it again. It's packed with her part-time work teaching at various schools and university summer math programs, as well as several writing and publishing credentials. Two local papers featured a prize-winning math essay of hers, but her initial university major was chemistry. She holds an annual mathematical festival for primary schoolchildren as part of her PhD work in computer science. She even has a YouTube channel of math jokes with three hundred subscribers.

But her profile picture really caught my attention. She wears glasses like me, drapes her long hair over her shoulders, and smiles like a beauty pageant winner—the phrase "sweet, but" sums her up perfectly. Perhaps she was thinking of a dirty math joke when the photo was taken?

I think I should feel flattered by Ms. Cheung's mention of my social media presence, yet the email conversation seems just a little bit off. But my father, an entrepreneur, emphasises the value of networking, and to me, any respectable person is worth connecting with. On top of that, I have a soft spot for naturally beautiful girls. I reply:

Wednesday, August 16, 2017 10:05 AM

Dear Ms. Cheung,

Thank you for your submission. We will review it and get back to you in due course.

If you wish to contact me personally, you may email me at prospernghk@gmail.com.

Best regards,
Prosper Ng

Only now do I download Alyson's attachment. My cursor doesn't move. After a few moments, another dialog box appears. This time it's an animated image of a beating heart. *Le sigh.* What's up with computers these days? There must be something wrong with its updates because this is the second time something like this has happened…

I restart my laptop. My cursor can move again. No kissing lips or beating hearts this time. Fine. I shake my head violently, as if I'm a wet dog trying to dry itself. I often watch YouTube prank videos, but that doesn't mean I like mischief to play out in real life.

Now I reopen Alyson's attachment. Nothing strange. I read Alyson's article and wince. It opens with a quote of the artist M. C. Escher… I've seen this name before!

The article then describes various tilings and discusses the three regular polygonal tilings using triangles, squares, and hexagons, supplemented with equations. Haven't I just discussed with someone else how to structure a tessellation article in such a way? How did Alyson come up with it? Her previous articles—all rejected—never approached such a topic.

Finally, the article touches upon Escher's tiling artwork. The good thing is, Alyson's piece reads like it's written by a teenager for her peers, a feeling I struggle to capture myself because I often sound too mature. I'm sure Damien will want this article too, and I'll make him happy with this little bit of delegation that I've done.

Still shocked by the similarity of her paper to the idea I'd recently had, I locate my email to Wanda describing the framework I gave her and re-read the article by Alyson. A prickly chill spirals up my spine. How could Alyson have adhered so closely to the outline I provided Wanda unless…

I read the headers of their emails, but I can't find any link between them. Could Wanda and Alyson know each other somehow? Could they even be the same person? I could ask my friends for help, but they might be too busy to play detective.

The next morning, I lie awake in bed and tap my phone. Alyson has reached me through email. I sense that I can befriend a respectable young lady while waiting for the chance to learn if she is being cunning with her MOQ submission. Best of both worlds.

We talk about math and economics for a start. (Online) dating 101: make a girl feel comfortable. Later, I can ask her if she's actually Wanda.

***

A month later, I'm lying in bed, enjoying an early morning conversation on how math is used in economic models with my secret online date before I attend to my MOQ email duties. We've graduated from email to WhatsApp so that we can communicate more quickly.

Tuesday, September 19, 2017 08:08 AM
Alyson: I've been wondering about something for a while. In Hong Kong your surname is supposed to be Wong, not Ng. Why the weirdness?

I scratch my head, looking for a simple explanation. Actually, "Ng" in Hong Kong is the Cantonese equivalent of the Chinese surname "Wu", but I'm not of Cantonese ancestry, unlike most Hongkongers. My surname is one of the non-Cantonese variants of "Wong".

I don't want her to suspect that I'm cautious about her, so I try to sound friendly.

Tuesday, September 19, 2017 08:10 AM
Me: I will need to ask my grandfather…

I send a message to my grandpa, who lives in Hong Kong.

Me: Grandpa, why are we Ngs instead of Wongs?

Grandpa is retired and spends a lot of time on his smartphone, messaging friends and family, so I'm not surprised at his prompt response.

Grandpa Ng: Blame the Immigration Department.

I shoot Alyson a quick response:

Me: The English transliteration of my surname was coined by the HK Immigration Department staff when my grandfather got his ID document many years ago. I suppose the transliteration practice was not so standardized back then.

Alyson: I see. That makes sense.

I smile. I'm glad she brought up my name—this is the perfect time to approach her about something that's been bothering me.

Me: I have a question for you. It might seem a bit odd, though.

Alyson: What is it?

Me: The essay you submitted to MOQ… Where did you get the idea?

Alyson: It just came to me one day. You liked it, right? When do I hear if it's accepted?

My smile shifts to a frown. I still can't be sure if she borrowed the idea from Wanda, or if she used an alias to get the idea from me. I haven't been able to find Wanda online beyond a private Facebook page with a doodle for a profile picture, but that doesn't mean anything. Not all math lovers are in the spotlight like I often am.

I can still try one more thing, though.

Me: Not for a few more weeks. The senior editor doesn't have a lot of time to review submissions, and he has to approve it.

She doesn't reply, but I get the sense that she's probably disappointed by my response—at least, I would be. I drum up the courage for one more try.

Me: One more odd question… Do you know someone named Wanda Norton?

Alyson: Doesn't ring a bell. Why?

What the—! I scramble to find a good answer.

Me: Never mind. Someone mentioned her name to me, but I didn't recognize it.

We resume chatting about math and economics. But deep down, I feel like she's more distant than before.

***

Friday, October 13, 2017 09:58 AM
Alyson: Being high-profile… What started it all?

Me? High-profile? I've only appeared on a smattering of papers as the subject of a news report or a commentator and given talks in person, over the radio, and on television shows. I once gave a glowing video testimonial for a math celebrity tutor, although I've never had to take tuition classes myself. My books on recreational math topics made their debut appearance during last year's Hong Kong Book Fair. We advertise them on social media as well. Even my Facebook feed asks me if I want to buy them…

Getting press coverage seems so normal to me that I've probably taken it for granted, and I admit that I enjoy the attention other people give me when I mention my public appearances and books.

We're quite friendly with each other now, so maybe I can say something to let down her guard, and then I'll press her again regarding her relationship with Wanda. It still disturbs me how much her article resembles the one I suggested.

Me: What makes you think I'm high-profile? :p

My fingers fidget, stroking the stubble on my chin. Being admired by the fairer sex gives me a floating sensation.

Alyson: You've spoken on TV and appeared on an advertisement recommending a star tutor. You've made public speeches many times. You've connected with the highest echelons of society, and you even have your own column in a local newspaper. Heck, you're even a published author. To me, a virtual wall separates me from people like you. I've wondered since childhood why some other boys and girls make it on TV or into the press (while I've made goofs when I was interviewed back then—hahahahaha). When did your exposure to the media all begin?

I should not answer this directly as it would give away the fact that my father, a rockstar businessman, has friends in high places too. A lot of it is down to my dad's efforts. It's just perfect that he has super connections, and I'm a high achiever…

Me: TV stations, schools, and people in society have probably come to know of me because of my academic endeavors. And some have read my column and books.

Man, I want to take back what I've just entered. It sounds too awkward, and I'm feeling embarrassed about the way I've come across.

Alyson: You're being modest. Your father is the executive of a tech company and he uses his connections to help you succeed.

I cringe. My brain screams "stalker, stalker". She's like a bee circling around me as if to sting me anytime. I need to know if she's Wanda, but she seems to think I'm an idiot.

Alyson: It doesn't matter to me how you got famous. Could we be Facebook friends?

On reading this line, my lungs have trouble drawing in air. It's like being thrust into a plastic bag that's tied up right away, leaving me to suffocate inside.

Me: I need to go now. Talk to you later.

Alyson: How about LinkedIn? You haven't added me as a connection yet!

Me: I can't add you.

Alyson: :(Why?

I roll up my sleeves, ready to snatch my normal routine back from her. Time to be blunt—and formal:

Me: I have no comment.

Knitting my brows together, I busy myself with other mobile apps. To my chagrin, Alyson eventually replies.

Alyson: What do you mean by "no comment"? It's very rude, you know, for people to say "no comment" in dealing with public relations! Don't think I'm making this up; I've been a student reporter before, and we hate such responses from bureaucrats. Didn't your father teach you not to say that?

Look, I'm also a math writer. I study math and computer science like you do. I have experience in the arts, and I share your passion for education. I also have a strong social media following, with 500 followers each on Twitter and Instagram. That means we can help each other succeed.

My computer science professor told me that 500 is the average number of followers on any social media platform, so this girl shouldn't brag. I have twenty times more followers than her on Facebook, Twitter, and Instagram combined.

That said, my followers are mostly strangers. Alyson's liked and followed me on all three platforms. She's not the only one who has done so, but she's the first to remember everything about me so well. Her constant attention is starting to scare me. I have to run and hide somehow, but where can I go? I can't just demote myself from social butterfly to hermit!

Friday, October 13, 2017 10:51 AM
Alyson: You seriously should friend me on Facebook. Your mum thought you didn't like her cooking; my mum thought I didn't like hers either. But we both eat the best food last. We could tell them both that, together. :)

My heart catches in my throat as if I'm going to cough it out by accident.

Eating the best food last—that was something I've only mentioned on my private Facebook posts, which she shouldn't have been able to read.

I bite my nails and pace to and fro in my room. Confront her? Ignore her?

I need to calm down. I sit in my swivel chair and spin round and round, trying to dull the feeling of being overwhelmed. How can she know so much about me when I know so little about her?

***

In stolen moments during class and lunch, I scramble for the appropriate words to write back to her. Maybe I should say, "You are such an annoying person." But this may encourage her to write back to defend herself.

My phone buzzes.

Friday, October 13, 2017 01:21 PM
Alyson: I've been groomed to be a lady since I was small. I remember you wrote in another article that you would love to have a wife who's ladylike and loves homeschooling just like you do. You surely can revisit my LinkedIn profile. I'm only a little older than you, and you mentioned that you like slightly older girls. I am yours.

I slam my phone face down. Now she's even throwing herself at my feet.

Later, another message pops up:

Friday, October 13, 2017 01:34 PM
Alyson: I don't normally tell people this, but I'll confide in you because I like you. I have Asperger's Syndrome.
I know you're busy. I'm sorry to have bothered you, but please, please, please reply. Your kindness is deeply appreciated.

Instantly, I close the chat window. Desperate girls are unattractive. I think I'll just ignore her and cross my fingers, hoping that she gets the idea and doesn't haunt me again.

I tap on the Facebook icon and come across posts by Joyce and Betty, on which Alyson has commented. More than the need to know whether Alyson is Wanda, I need to be safe, so I'm looking for someone on good terms with Alyson to persuade her to back off.

It's nearing time to head to my next class. I make my way to the lecture hall, resolving to message Joyce and Betty once I grab a seat.

The lecture hall has no windows, so when the lights are off, it's frighteningly dark. However, the class before mine has left the lights on. I'm early. Class will start at two.

Alone, I sit in the front row and reach out to Joyce first on WhatsApp.

Friday, October 13, 2017 01:43 PM
Me: What can you tell me about Alyson Cheung?

Joyce: I don't want to talk about her.

Me: I've been getting disturbing messages from her. Can you tell her to stop?

I take out my notes to read them. The lights suddenly go off. I turn on the flashlight app on my phone. Maybe it's just a glitch, a temporary power outage.

I wait with bated breath. The lights don't turn on.

With the flashlight on my phone, I approach the switch and flip it. The lights are now on.

It's the same empty hall again. Why did the lights go off? Could it be a trick by a hidden student? I check each of the desks. Nobody is hiding. Phew. I return to my seat.

Once I plop myself down on my seat, the lights turn off again!

I rub my eyes, wondering what's going on. Perhaps I should sit outside so that when the professor comes, I can tell him the lights aren't working. But I need to make sure my experience is not a delusion.

Holding up my phone, I return to the switch and turn on the lights again. This time, I hold the switch down. The lights shine behind me.

I finally lift my finger—the lights turn off again. A curse slips out as I flip the light switch up and down repeatedly. But the lights don't respond to me. Instead, they flicker repeatedly of their own accord, long and short flashes interspersing each other. I think I know something about these…

I faintly smell something singed. Could it be that the light circuits are getting overheated? I sprint away from the lecture hall with my notes, holding my breath.

Time ticks away on my watch as I observe the hall from outside the entrance. The long flashes last for 1 second. The short flashes take up about half a second. Is it…Morse code?

I grab a pen and jot down how long the light lasts before it's off again:

.--- . - .---- .- .. -- . .--- . - .---- .- .. -- . .--- . - .---- .- .. -- .

It's looping the phrase *Je t'aime*, which is French for "I love you". This is freaking me out so much that I'm on the verge of peeing in my pants. The only person I know who's infatuated with me now is Alyson, and there's no way she could be behind this. Right? It has to be some student's prank. I take a deep breath and grip my pen, ready to attack with it anytime.

I've not been this scared since the first time I had a horde of paparazzi surrounding me on my way to school. I tried to hide my face, but they kept snapping pictures of me. The white flashes were blinding. I took off running and the entire drove followed me. Once I got to school, I locked myself in the washroom and called my father, who identified the offending gossip magazines and put a restraining order on them. I was only eleven.

I take a deep breath and turn on the lights. My finger stays pressed on the switch. They stay on.

I lift my finger. The lights are still on.

Taking a seat at a desk, I refocus on my class notes. I try to breathe normally. For a moment, I close my eyes, then I open them again. The lights are still…on. But I can still smell what I think is the burnt circuit.

Other students begin to fill the lecture hall.

"Smell anything strange?" I ask them.

They shake their heads. I sit. Telling them about the lights as well would be a worse idea.

Dr. Harry Watson, the economics teacher as well as my thesis supervisor, enters. He prefers that I call him Harry. This is a graduate-level class. I take notes as soon as he speaks. When Harry takes a break to drink some water, my phone buzzes in my pocket.

Friday, October 13, 2017 02:12 PM
Joyce: No. That vicious hacker and I are not friends anymore.

Hacker… So Alyson's a computer hacker. The coincidences between my emails to Wanda and Alyson's math article, as well as the havoc on my computer and this classroom soon after our conversations. If only I could nail down the evidence, maybe I could get a restraining order on her as well.

I post on Facebook that I need help concerning a series of hacking incidents. Instantly I get seventy likes. Many of them comment, "Take care!" But I'm not asking for condolences—I. Need. Help.

Betty seems to be friendlier to Alyson in their Facebook conversations. So I message Betty:

Friday, October 13, 2017 02:36 PM

Me: I don't want to regret sounding too blunt when I'm not happy. Please tell Alyson Cheung nicely that I do not intend to talk to her again.

I turn back to the professor, who's filled half of the board with letters, arithmetic symbols, and arrows. I copy them furiously. My phone buzzes. I pick it up.

Friday, October 13, 2017 02:49 PM
Betty: I'll try, but no guarantees. Has she been threatening you in any way?

Me: No threats, just harassment. I need this to stop now.

Alyson strikes again, this time on Facebook. Shame on me for forgetting to block her. With anger boiling in my chest, I skim her latest message.

Friday, October 13, 2017 03:06 PM
Alyson: I seriously like you. All I care is that you're everything I've ever wanted in a boyfriend: the man who is "known in the gates, when he sits among the elders of the land." (Proverbs 31:23) And you've written that you consider Christian girls very good at this link: www.prosperng.hk/my-views-on-religion. Since you live abroad, I think you know how to cook. That would be fantastic because I see your food pictures and they look scrumptious. 'Nuff said. I'm yours.

My finger hovers over the "delete conversation" button, but I stop myself. I would be eradicating potentially incriminating evidence. I know it's a bit unfair to get Betty involved, but my interactions with Alyson before she got mad were pleasant. I don't want to complain directly to Alyson and make her think I'm a jerk.

I message Betty again:

Friday, October 13, 2017 03:13 PM

Me: Would you please tell Alyson that human relationships are not like math problems? Persistence will land her in prison.

I scribble on my loose sheets of paper, trying hard to catch up with Harry.

Class is dismissed at 03:30 PM sharp. I check my phone.

Friday, October 13, 2017 03:29 PM
Betty: Done. She should leave you alone now. Should.

Betty: But you still have to be careful.

Of course, of course. Alyson's a computer hacker. My friends high and low can only give me the hackneyed and unseemly phrase, "Take care." Who else can I turn to for help?

I line up at the nearest dining hall, grab my salad, and find an empty table. Overwhelmed by frustration, I pull out my phone as if it's a good-luck charm. Three more messages from Betty.

Friday, October 13, 2017 03:32 PM
Betty: Alyson's confided in me that she used to exploit a bug in an English learning platform to get the top grade.

Friday, October 13, 2017 03:34 PM
Betty: She also once had an internship carrying out online surveys, but she cheated the system by doing the surveys herself, presenting similar responses. She was fired from the job, and she never put it on her resume.

Friday, October 13, 2017 03:37 PM
Betty: Joyce won't speak with Alyson anymore after she stole our email addresses and created a forged email conversation between the two of us. We reported this criminal incident to the IT services center at our

university, but we can't prove she's behind it because we couldn't find any evidence. She's a master at hiding her tracks, but thank your lucky stars she's become careless. I got her to spill her criminal history after a bit of prodding just now.

My jaw drops, but I cover my mouth.

***

I don't miss Alyson, even though she has not contacted me for days. The air is getting cooler outside, and I snuggle in my blanket while I study.

Taking a break from my homework, I check my email. Good grief! Damien's given her article the green light. I'd forgotten to tell him what happened.

Tuesday, October 17, 2017 10:16 AM
Me: I don't think we should publish Alyson Cheung's article. She's been stalking me.

Damien: How so?

Me: She bombards me with messages saying she loves me. I can show you.

Damien: I have to remind you that our editorial policy is not biased on a personal basis. So whatever grievance you have, you have to act professionally. Since her article is suitable for our audience, you cannot dismiss it just because she's wronged you somehow.

I hope I don't come across as too harsh. Perhaps she still has some goodness in her and you don't see it yet. You must treat people the way you want to be treated.

Damien's preachiness is the bane of my existence. Duh…

I protect myself with the official MOQ editor email address.

Tuesday, October 17, 2017 10:37 AM
Re: Submission

Dear Ms. Cheung,

We plan to use your submission titled "The Many-Splendored Tessellations" in the seventh issue of MOQ, which will be published in March 2018, subject to some edits.

Reserving the right to request further edits, we would like to know if you consent to the edits shown in the attached file.

Please also let us know whether you are willing to translate the edited version into Chinese.

Thank you.

Best regards,
Editorial Board of MOQ

I attach her article containing my comments and hit "Send".

At night, I check my email. That stalker has replied, but not addressing it to the "Editorial Board of MOQ" directly. It's my fault my comments on her submission all had my name attached to them.

Tuesday, October 17, 2017 06:22 PM

Dear Mr. Ng,

I consent to all the edits, I will send you my Chinese translation this week, and I anticipate our collaboration.

Best regards,
Alyson Cheung

I sneer at her formality. She's trying to trick me into feeling good about her again. Recalling the two prank dialog boxes, I mutter under my breath, loosely quoting *A Midsummer Night's Dream*, "'I love thee not, therefore pursue me not.' 'Hence, get thee gone, and follow me no more.'"

Everything on my monitor disappears in a flash. I yelp. "Argh!" I press all the keys on my keyboard frantically.

Nothing happens. I cover my eyes in denial. I don't want to believe that my computer is finished.

I gather myself. What's done is done. I grunt at the computer, certain that Alyson is listening. "'Tempt not too much the hatred of my spirit; / For I am sick when I do look on thee.'"

In reply, a faint, girly voice emits from the computer and speaks melodramatically, "'And I am sick when I look *nooooooooot* on you.'"

The screen bleeds into a red background. I glare at the empty white dialog box fading in. I tilt my head, and to my horror, it tilts in the direction of my head... I cover the laptop camera with my thumb, and the dialog box stops moving.

Crooked handwritten words surface letter by letter from the dialog box. "Your hard disk is encrypted, your data will be erased, and your bank account will be emptied in 24 hours, unless you pay me...your love."

To hell with Shakespeare. I growl, "I. Will. Not!" I slam the laptop shut.

I take a few more breaths and open it again. The dialog box is gone, but the red screen remains. Stupid of me not to have taken a snapshot with my phone.

I rush to the computer laboratory and freeze my bank account first. I also bring my laptop to a graduate student who's a part-time technician.

Finishing today's work, my thesis included, at the computing lab is a breeze. Thank goodness I saved everything on Dropbox, and I'm using hard copies of my textbooks.

At the end of the twenty-four hours, the technician says he can't reboot my computer anymore. Thankfully, my money is safe in the bank. I'll need to buy a new laptop, though.

***

I'm afraid of checking my emails now because I keep getting emails from "myself" detailing my Facebook posts. Because of them, I finally block Alyson this morning—my Facebook log indicates that she never logged into my account directly, so I don't have to change my password. I'm fed up with her.

Alone in my dorm room—a single room—I lose track of the passing hours, buried in my tomes, until my phone rings on my bedside table. I pick it up and squint at the unknown number displayed. It's a US number, perhaps from the California area. I let it ring. I hope it's just another cold caller who'll tick my name off when I don't respond.

The ringing doesn't stop. It could be someone important. I recall Dad's admonition to connect with people. Five more rings later, I pick up the call.

"Who's this?" I snap, a bit disappointed that it has interrupted my lovely plan to study.

"Is this Prosper Ng?" asks an enthusiastic voice. "My name is…" The connection isn't great—I think it's a male name, but whoever it is sounds harmless enough.

"That's true. Where are you calling from?"

"From Hong Kong!" says the dude gleefully.

I gasp. This is definitely not a Hong Kong number. How is this guy using a US number to call from Hong Kong? I could hang up, but I want to seize the opportunity to unmask the identity of the caller myself. Perhaps the police can trace this number.

The mystery caller continues, "I'm using Google Voice to call you because all US numbers are free. It's a Gmail feature." At this point he sounds hysterical. "Didn't you know that?"

I don't know how to answer. A prank call in the morning is something I least expected. But I have a sneaking suspicion that this person is not really a man.

"I was thinking of sending you an email, but decided to call instead."

Sending me an email… I have a hunch this guy is in fact the dreadful Alyson in disguise. I quietly ask, "Where did you find my number?"

"From the economics blog of Dr. Harry Watson," he says, still cheery. "I'm an economics postgraduate who's going to MIT later this month, and I stumbled across his post of your upcoming talk at Kresge Auditorium."

This doesn't fit what I know about Alyson, but it could just be another alias she's made up. But unless I know who the caller really is, I won't hang up. The police can't solve cases where there's insufficient evidence. I must take matters into my own hands. Just like writing for MOQ myself.

"Why are you calling?" I snap.

"Because I want to sign up for your talk."

The talk he is referring to is the public seminar accompanying my thesis. I shake my head in shame. I wish I hadn't persuaded my supervisor to promote my talk. It has just attracted unwanted attention. But it's too late to take it down now.

I speak quickly and professionally. "It's a walk-in talk."

"Oops, sorry," he says, sounding mildly annoyed.

"Do you know how to get to Kresge Auditorium?"

"I know the way, thanks, pal. By the way, what do you study at MIT, *young gent?*"

I hide my snigger at his abruptly antiquated manner of speaking. If he's really read the seminar poster, he should know the answer. Maybe it isn't Alyson after all, just some absentminded postgrad. "I study math," I say, rolling my eyes upwards, "and I'm interested in economics."

"That's very nice—"

I hurl at him the dreaded question. "Are you Alyson?"

Silence. I hear him inhaling, his nasal sound reaching a climax, then silence.

I cannot waste my time waiting. "I've got to go now." I hang up. Immediately, I send voice messages to my parents, my grandparents, and Damien about my new encounter. This madness has to end.

"She calls you because she's desperate for your attention," my grandfather says. "You'd better call the police."

Dad simply says, "Stay away from her."

But will she stay away from me?

"The only way to indict her is to document this new evidence," Damien says. Stupid of me not to have recorded that phone call. I have posted on Facebook about the incidents happening to me, but I'm the only witness. It's depressing to make claims without adequate support.

In the afternoon, I get a text message from my bank:

Thursday, October 19, 2017 02:01 PM

Dear Prosper Ng,

Our bank has detected suspicious activity with your account. A sum of $3000.00 was withdrawn from your account at 01:57 PM on October

19, 2017. Please call a representative at 555 875 0050 to review and verify this activity…

I've been manipulated for so long, and I loathe myself for it. But what can I do? Dialog boxes can be ignored, and malware can be stopped, but the disappearing evidence? Am I making up everything I've experienced so far? Now she's even taken my money. Why?

I call the bank. When I finally get to speak to a live member of staff, I tell him that the 3,000 dollars was a theft. He tells me that the bank will reimburse me in ten business days. Standard processing times suck.

***

The next day, at 10 PM, I'm sitting on my bed in my dorm room. There's no moon outside, and I realize I'm looking at nothingness over my left shoulder. An 1892 article "Folk-Lore from Maine," which I came across a few days ago, claims this pose brings bad luck—how unscientific.

I scroll through my email from my phone, expecting nothing special. I freeze. Why is Damien's email in the MOQ editors' inbox? He usually writes to my personal address. Gingerly, I tap on it.

Friday, October 20, 2017 07:09 PM

Dear Mr. Ng,

I was quite surprised to receive your email but, as I've said before, I have no plans to be interviewed by MOQ or any other Hong Kong publication. I studied abroad and only when I returned to Hong Kong did I learn of the local curriculum. I cannot provide much advice for secondary school students, unless I repeat what others have told me, when it comes to juggling examination and recreational math. I hope this is a good answer for you.

Best regards,
Damien Fu

I scroll down, to my shock and horror.

Dear Prof. Fu,

I noticed that I haven't had the chance to interview you even though you're part of MOQ. Would you be willing to share what you know with Hong Kong students?

Best regards,
Prosper Ng

I bang my fists on the table. I know I didn't write that enclosed email.

I double-check my "Sent" folder. It's not there.

It must be that girl. Joyce warned me about her. Betty confided in me about her past. What would that witch get out of pretending to be me? She must, must, must pay for her crimes.

On my phone, I carefully type up an email to Alyson, trying my best to refuse her in the politest way possible:

Saturday, October 21, 2017 02:02 AM
Information and request

Dear Ms. Cheung,

I should wish to record that when you first messaged me months ago to discuss intellectual questions, I replied several times. Then you made increasingly explicit romantic suggestions, but I have no interest in this matter with reference to you, so I ceased to respond. Now and at all future times, I do not wish to engage in any personal communication with you, whether intellectual or not, regardless of your intent.

I hope that you will respect my wish not to be contacted personally by you on any platform, by any means, and in any name. Emphatically, please do not reply to the present email. I would also like to request that you not hurt yourself or anyone else in any fashion as a result of my respectful declination.

Yours sincerely,
Prosper Ng

I spent too long constructing this email. I hit "Send" on my phone, tuck myself into bed, and plop my head against the pillow. I message Damien about the forgery.

I close my eyes. If that mean girl has any common sense, she won't dare retaliate.

***

I have a dreamless sleep. In the morning, I wake up and check my phone—10:03 AM—only to locate an email by the alumni association of my old secondary school.

Saturday, October 21, 2017 03:09 AM

Dear Mr. Ng,

We're delighted to have you as a keynote speaker during the summer. Do let us know what your topic is by May 5.

Best regards,
Stephanie Tung (Ms.)
St. Urban College Alumni Association, Hong Kong

—Friday, October 20, 2017 10:54 PM GMT -0500 Prosper Ng <prospernghk@gmail.com>:—

Dear Ms. Tung,

I wish to join the career talk on June 30. Please provide me with details. Thank you for your kind attention, and I look forward to your prompt response.

Best regards,
Prosper Ng

I know Ms. Tung—she's a teacher and a good friend of mine. As I read the quoted "original," my fingers tremble. I would have returned to my school if I had willingly written that email, but I didn't.

I reply, gritting my teeth:

Saturday, October 21, 2017 10:03 AM

Dear Ms. Tung,

The email you received from "me" is forged. I have never asked to be a part of this career event. I kindly request to be removed from further communications regarding this matter and would like you to report this incident to the police, as I am not in Hong Kong.

Yours sincerely,
Prosper Ng

Another email—I'm now getting wary of senders' email addresses:

From: harry@harrywatsonloveseconomics.com
To: prospernghk@gmail.com
Saturday, October 21, 2017 03:04 AM
Welcome to Harry Watson's Economics Blog

I'll follow thee and make a heaven of hell,

To die upon the hand I love so well.

As I've been a longtime subscriber of his blog, there's absolutely no reason for him to re-welcome me. Nor is his welcome email anything like this one—he doesn't quote Shakespeare in it. This is creepy—I forward the email to Harry. In short, he says that he's shocked and he's asked the webmaster to investigate the matter.

***

The next day, I receive another email:

From: prospernghk@gmail.com
To: prospernghk@gmail.com
Sunday, October 22, 2017 05:01 AM
Math is lovely

Sine says to Cosine, "Shall we Tangent or Cotangent?"

Oh my goodness. I can't help blushing. This girl is cracking a dirty math joke—simply put, Sine and Cosine are two people asking who should lie on top of the other.

I report this anomaly to the Hong Kong Police through their online reporting form, along with as much supporting evidence as I can scrape together from my email accounts and social apps. I type out as much as I can remember about Wanda and Alyson, as well as the descriptions of the computer attacks I've experienced.

I click the "Submit" button.

Two hours later, the police redirect me to the FBI, as it solves crimes that cross international borders. I hurry to the nearest local FBI office with both my laptops, the hacked one and the new one. I also tell Thompson, the officer handling my case, about Alyson's past in hacking, showing him Betty's conversation with me. I leave my hacked laptop with him and let him copy my conversations regarding Alyson.

***

I dropped off my laptop a week ago. Even though I've since met lawyers, members of law enforcement, and IT experts, they tell me that the criminal behind it is so skilled, it appears that I was the one doing all the crazy things I claimed she did to my computers. I don't think so.

Now, I'm angrily-frustratedly-busily forwarding to the FBI Alyson's pseudonymous emails as they come. The addresses they're sent from are becoming increasingly worrisome: iloveyou@wanttogettogether.now, please@be-mine.now, soonyouwill@loveme.too, and even prospernghk @hasanonlinegirlfriend.now.

On Friday, I meet Officer Thompson again. I hope he can point the finger at Alyson. But he says, "The Hong Kong Police managed to reach Ms. Alyson Cheung, who maintained her silence through a solicitor. We've found out that the offending emails and malware originated from your infected computer. It appears that there's been a misunderstanding, and no one has been harmed."

What? No…

***

All weekend, I keep getting emails from more bogus addresses. I just delete them out of frustration because there's nothing else I can do. Although I keep changing my email addresses and updating my passwords, the accounts still get hacked. I've tried everything.

On Monday, I meet my supervisor Harry for the last time before my presentation and I mention my mishaps. A former computer science student himself, he tells me that he read a guest blog post this morning that explained that emails can be sent without having to verify the sender's identity using anonymous mailing techniques available to anyone tech-savvy. Even if the FBI knew about this post, they might find it hard to pin down the real author.

We use his laptop to look up the blog and its Whois entry, which reveals that the website is not based in Hong Kong or the US. But its writing style sounds like that in Alyson's tessellation article—sweet, but.

I hate being taunted outright.

***

It's about noon on Tuesday, November 7, 2017. Tomorrow's the day I present my thesis—way ahead of time because I'm terrified of that girl. I'm a boy, and I should be stronger than her, but she really freaks me out. Right after the seminar, I'm taking a flight home to Hong Kong to sign the papers for Alyson's restraining order. I've packed almost everything.

Ambling outside my dorm looking for a good eatery, I receive a phone call from an unknown US number. It could be Alyson, so I activate a phone conversation recording app. Only then do I pick it up.

"Hello?" I ask.

"Dr. Harry Watson is now unconscious outside the Warehouse," says a rapid female voice. The Warehouse is another dorm, for first-year graduate students. Usually around this time, Harry is out, so if I call or email him, he can't reply immediately. "You must hand over—"

My phone beeps—it's running out of battery. A ponytailed girl holds a phone against her ear further down the path. I dash to her and grab her arm. "Help me," I tell her. "My supervisor has fainted outside the Warehouse. Can you call Urgent Care?"

She dials on her phone, head down. I frown, watching her. Her face looks strangely familiar.

"Hello," she says. "Is this Urgent Care? Yes, we have—" She has the same rapid voice as the caller just now.

"Where's Dr. Watson?" I shout.

She rushes forward and kicks me in the groin. I clutch myself and bend forward. A faint hiss reaches my ear. Droplets sear my forehead with pain. I try to wipe them off, but now my hand hurts too. I've just been sprayed with who-knows-what.

I vaguely recall that Alyson has studied chemistry. "What did you do to me?"

She grabs my chin, yanking my face to hers and forcing me to gaze at her. My lungs want to protest as I inhale her sickly sweet smell, but my eyes are already growing heavy. Weights tug at them, urging me to nod off. I want to slap her, but my hand droops instead. She crushes her body into mine, kissing me deeply.

I feel like vomiting and I try, try, try to keep my eyes open, but I can't. She whispers in my favorite language, "*N'agacez pas une fille amoureuse.*" Don't offend a girl in love.

She releases me. My head spins violently as a dizzying darkness overtakes me.

***

A year goes by. The restraining order is signed, and Alyson has left me alone completely. I'm relieved. Although her article was published, Damien and I co-wrote the entirety of the final issue of MOQ because of her incident. Life is finally back to normal.

Amidst the praise I receive from friends for the success of MOQ are congratulations and even prayers for me as a new *father*. Confused yet certain Alyson is behind this, I Google her.

Her baby boy looks just like me in infancy.

The Solstice Beast

Katelyn Barbee

It sensed her at the edge of the woods, roused from its deep slumber by the old magic. It wiggled its way out from beneath the roots of the oak that had been its den this past year before slipping into the shade, where the light could not touch it.

The girl's head snapped up, eyes rounder than full moons and more frightened than those of the dying deer beside her. Her gaze darted from tree to tree then to her car parked by the curb of the deserted road. "Who's there?"

Slowly, it receded into the snow-heavy branches.

Patience.

Night would come soon, and it would be free from its bindings once again.

***

Morgan pressed her phone to her ear for the fifth time, her warm breath coming out in quick puffs, clouding the chilly air. Her heart slammed against her ribcage, body shivering. "Come on, please, pick up."

Of all the days to hit a deer, it had to be this one. She glanced back at the front of her mom's beat-up old car and winced. The right headlight flickered, as if someone was sending out a Morse code, then went out. Blood streaked across the white, half-wrinkled hood. Chunks of tissue and tufts of fur coated the caved-in grille. *Mom's going to kill me.*

She shuddered, gaze settling on the setting sun just beyond the forested hills. The back of her neck prickled as she drew in a shaky, frigid breath.

"Morgan? What's up?"

She startled, nearly dropping her phone at the crackle of Allan's voice.

Thank God. "I need help," she bit out.

"What's wrong?" His tone was sharp, concerned.

"I hit a deer."

"Are you okay?"

"Fine, just shaken." She checked over her shoulder, glancing down the curve of frozen, empty highway. "Look, I can't get ahold of anybody else. The calls won't go through. Can you—"

"Where are you?"

Morgan swallowed, the back of her dry throat sticking. "A couple miles from the tunnel."

Allan mumbled something to someone, probably his twin sister, Hanna—they were practically conjoined, never one without the other—and then asked, "Do you think you can drive the car at all?"

"It won't start—"

The deer let out a long, low moan. A flock of birds took flight in the distance, scattering into the cloudless sky.

Morgan's heart sank. Jagged white bone poked past the unfurling strands of tissue still clinging to its mangled legs. She stroked the soft fur between its ears, frowning. "I'm sorry. I didn't mean to hit you."

The line crackled.

"What?" Allan asked.

"I was talking to the deer..." She frowned and kneeled next to it, gazing into its soft, glassy eyes. "It's not dead."

"Then you should put it out of its misery. Cruel not to."

"I can't," she choked. She couldn't even squash bugs. How was she supposed to be able to finish off a deer? It wasn't like she had anything with her that would do the job, either.

Jets of hot air warmed Morgan's legs as its bloody chest rose and fell, quivering and glistening in the golden sun sinking behind snowy hills painted eerie blue by the growing shadows. Another half an hour and it would be completely dark.

"Alright," Allan said. "Give me ten minutes, and I'll be—"

The phone cut off.

She stared at it. Lost signal blinked across the screen.

"God dammit." She shoved her phone into a pocket so she wouldn't be tempted to chuck it against a tree. "Useless piece of crap."

She glanced over her shoulder again. Her skin prickled. She'd heard fearful whispers at school about a ghost or monster living in the woods, but no one would tell her exactly what it was, something Hanna planned to remedy tonight. Or maybe it was just her overactive imagination and the newness of being outside in the woods. Not to mention the snow and the cold. Living in LA, she'd never had to worry about it, but here... *Maybe I should go wait in the car...just to be safe.*

Headlights flashed up the road as a pickup truck came around the sharp bend. It slowed, parking twenty feet behind Morgan's car. *Oh good, maybe they can help.*

A door slammed and a silhouette—she couldn't tell if it was a man or woman because they wore so many layers—cut across the headlights, heavy boots crunching through the snow toward her. Morgan eyed the hunting rifle slung across the figure's narrow shoulders and the heavy-looking knife on their belt. She'd been told hunters frequented the woods, but the gun's presence still unnerved her. *People are way too gun-happy here.*

"Need some help?" The voice was an old woman's, ancient and surprisingly gravelly, like her grandmother's rasp from decades of chain smoking.

Morgan stood, brushing the snow from her jeans and pea coat. She motioned to the deer. "It just came out of nowhere."

The woman, all frown lines and deep wrinkles, nodded grimly. "I'll take care of it."

"You will?"

The old woman knelt next to the poor creature, squinting up at Morgan. "What are you doing out here this late?"

"Late?" It was barely five o'clock.

"Yes. The woods." The old woman glanced toward the trees before her stare settled on Morgan again. "You shouldn't be out here, not on the solstice. Especially in the dark."

Solstice? Maybe she's the local weirdo Allan warned me about. "I was just on my way home," Morgan lied, failing to meet the woman's hardening gaze.

The woman removed her knife, and Morgan turned away. She flinched when she heard the knife slip into flesh and scrape against bone. The deer's ragged breathing cut off.

"Home? So not the underpass?" the woman said finally, her voice cutting like her blade.

"Yes," Morgan said, folding her arms across her chest, trying to rub some warmth back into them. She snuck a glance at the old woman as she hauled the deer into the back of her rusted pickup truck. "My friend's supposed to come pick me up."

The old woman eyed Morgan's vehicle before her gaze drifted over to the woods again. When she spoke, her voice was gruff. "I can help you with your car."

"No." Morgan shook her head, fighting to keep the trembling from her voice. "No, it's fine. He'll be here any minute."

The woman scrutinized her for a long moment then shrugged. "If you say so."

"I'm going to go wait in my car." Morgan quickly walked back to her car and hopped in, trying to keep her hands from shaking as she gripped the cold leather of the steering wheel. Her heart knocked against her ribs. She locked the doors, watching in the rearview mirror as the woman got back into her pickup.

After the woman left, Morgan dialed Allan again, but each attempt failed. She cursed under her breath. *So much for that.*

She sighed, sinking into her seat to wait. The minutes passed by achingly slow, the thin shadows of tree trunks growing long as the sun continued to sink below the horizon.

Ten minutes later, a familiar blue Ford Focus approached and parked in front of Morgan's car. Allan got out and jogged over to her, a few strands of his chestnut hair falling into his blue eyes.

She threw open her door. "Thank God, you're here."

He dropped into a smooth bow. When he glanced up, he flashed a warm smile that made Morgan melt a little inside. "Your carriage awaits, My Lady."

The knotted bundle of nerves in her belly slowly unfurled. She grinned as she climbed out of her car. *Maybe I should get stranded more often...*

He shut her door, jabbing his thumb at the scrunched hood. "You still want me to take a look?"

"No, we can come back for it tomorrow. Let's just go." *No way in hell I'm staying here any longer than I have to.*

"If that's what you want..." He jerked his head toward his car. "Come on, hop in."

Morgan buckled herself in as Allan's vehicle came to life. She held her hands out to the vents, letting the warm air blast her half-frozen fingers. "For a minute there, I thought I might have to walk the rest of the way. Thanks for getting me."

He laughed, one corner of his mouth quirking up. "Any time."

***

It followed the car down the road for several minutes until they parked, and the girl and her companion exited. They marched into the darkening woods, straight toward its home. Next to the boy, who was all broad shoulders and height, she looked small and birdlike. Breakable.

It would save her for last.

Oh, how it longed to breathe in the air with new lungs. To feel the cold prickle its warm flesh. To tear and bite and taste.

And it would.

Soon.

***

Morgan yelped as her foot caught a root, and she landed face first in the cold slush. Allan's deep laughter rang out behind her as she flipped onto her back and sat up. She shook the snow from her tangled red hair. "I hate this place."

He pulled her to her feet then slung his arm around her shoulders, beaming. "Aw, come on, it's not *that* bad here."

She shrugged off his arm, scowling as she slipped and stumbled through the snow. "Let's just get this over with."

"Morgan." He caught her hand, concern etched across his brow, blue gaze meeting hers. "Are you sure you're—"

"I'm fine." She pulled away, stuffing her numb fingers into her coat pockets. Her shoulders slumped. "Sorry, this place…it just freaks me out."

"If you really don't want to do this, I can talk with her." Allan nudged her arm gently. "Get her to understand."

"And have Hanna tell the entire school that the new girl chickened out? I don't think so." She trudged on. "Let's go."

By the time the two made it to the abandoned underpass, they were deep in the woods, the last rays on the purple horizon receded between the thin trees, the night creeping in. The bright flames of a campfire rose high into the chilly air at the tunnel's entrance.

A towering shadow flickered across the high, curving concrete walls, dwindling into petite Hanna, who danced wildly around the flames like some medieval witch summoning the Devil. Allan had warned her earlier in biology that Hanna liked being dramatic, but she'd thought he'd been exaggerating then. *Guess not.*

Hanna stopped suddenly, black hair whipping across her face as she turned to them. Her lips stretched back in a grin, her white smile almost unnaturally wide. "Decided to show up, did you? Good. We can start, then."

Morgan dropped down onto the rough, cracked asphalt next to Allan, holding her numb hands toward the glowing flames. "Just get on with it already," she said flatly. The faster they got this over with, the better.

Hanna and her stupid initiation rituals. But Hanna ran the school, and if it meant fitting in and making friends— something she'd never managed in LA despite her efforts— maybe it would be worth it. And then there was Allan. She'd only known him a couple of weeks, but she found his presence calming. *And he's attractive; how did I get so lucky?* Back home, a guy like him would've never looked her way, but here, with so few other girls her age around, she had a chance. Maybe moving to Hawthorne wasn't such a bad thing after all.

"While there's daylight left, Hanna." Allan stuck his hands under his armpits, shoulders rising. "It's already cold as hell out here, and we have class tomorrow."

Morgan bit back a smile. *Such a goody-two-shoes.*

"Calm down, Mr. Perfect Attendance." Hanna rolled her eyes. "You'll keep your record."

Allan grumbled something under his breath.

"Very well…" Hanna's indigo dress flared out as she sat on the other side of the fire. She leaned forward, hands pressed against her knees as she cleared her throat loudly then spoke in a dramatic voice, "Fifty years ago, on a night just like this, three teenagers went into the woods." She held up a finger. "Only one came out alive." She pointed to the pitch-black tunnel. "Two of them were found dead in the underpass, their hearts ripped from their chests, guts spilling out of their bellies."

Morgan made a face. "That's gross."

"Oh, it gets worse," Hanna said, her voice filled with relish. "The hearts hadn't just been ripped out; they'd been *eaten.*" She held out her hands and wiggled her fingers. "The police found the survivor covered in blood, two half-devoured hearts still clutched in her hands. Some say she'd gone insane, but we all know better. The thing in the woods made her do it."

Morgan shuddered. The deer…had it been trying to flee something? And the unseen eyes watching her from the woods. Maybe she hadn't imagined that. She'd—

Allan stared at her, mouth twisted with concern.

She untucked her hair from behind her ear, hiding behind the curtain it created as she glanced at him. "What?"

"Nothing." He turned to Hanna, face relaxing. "Are you going to finish or not?"

Hanna smirked, gesturing to them. "I will once you guys stop making goo-goo eyes."

"We weren't," Morgan and Allan said in unison, leaning away from each other.

"Whatever." Hanna shrugged. "Back to what I was saying. The thing in the woods. Some people say it's been here forever. That the tribe that lived on this land used to sacrifice people to it. Some say they worshiped it."

Allan scoffed. "You're telling it wrong. They never worshiped it."

"Fine." Hanna crossed her arms, chin raised. "Then you tell it."

Allan took a nearby branch and tossed it into the fire. Greedy flame tongues licked the offering, hissing and snapping in approval as shadows danced under Allan's eyes. His gaze met Morgan's. She looked away, heat building in her cheeks. She played with her earring, glancing back his way in time to see a smile creep onto his lips.

"Some say it was an annual thing," he said in such a soft voice that Morgan had to lean toward him to make out his words. "Others swear they went longer, sometimes decades, before having to perform the ritual again, but the purpose was always the same: to keep it at bay."

"So what is it exactly?" Morgan whispered.

Allan rubbed his hands together before holding them out toward the fire. "Most say it's a spirit. Maybe a demon. Some even think it's a Wendigo. No one knows exactly."

"All we know is it has a taste for human flesh." Hanna's red lips curled into a wicked smile. "And hearts. But—"

A sudden gust ripped through their makeshift camp, making the flames flare before tearing through the tunnel.

Morgan clutched her coat around her as the howling wind bit at her face and hands, pulling at her hair. A faint pink line rimmed the hills beyond them now, the last of the sunlight swallowed by the night. Soon it would be completely dark. "How much more of this story is there?"

"It's almost over," Allan reassured her. "We'll head back to my house afterward. You can call your stepdad. We can roast marshmallows and drink hot cocoa while you wait, if you want."

Morgan smiled. "Thanks. I'd like—"

Hanna groaned.

"What?" Allan's brow furrowed.

She glared at them. "Are you two going to keep interrupting me, or can I finish?"

"Go on, then." Allan motioned for her to continue. "We're waiting."

Hanna cleared her throat. "Where was I?"

"You were saying something about the thing in the woods eating hearts," Morgan prompted, shuddering.

"Right." Hanna nodded. "As I was saying, it—"

Footsteps crunched through the snow somewhere in the distance behind Morgan. Her heart raced, thudding in her ears. She glared at Hanna. "This isn't funny."

"It's not me, I swear." Hanna got to her feet, dusting off the snow clinging to her black leggings. She wrapped her arms around herself. "Hello?" Her voice wavered, devoid of its usual confidence.

Nothing.

Allan stood abruptly, his mouth in a thin line. "Cut the act. Who is it? Desmond? Janie?"

The shuffling footsteps grew closer and closer.

Hanna's eyes widened in fear. "I promise it's not me this time!"

A dark silhouette appeared between the trees.

***

It waited in the mouth of the tunnel as the old huntress emerged from the shadows and began to shout at the two girls and the boy. Too late. She was too late. The night had come, and it would take whomever it pleased.

It raced at the nearest one, the dark-haired girl, slipping in past slightly parted lips to sink its hooks deep into her brain and become one. Hanna. Her name was Hanna. It burrowed deeper. The boy. Allan. Brother. Wombmate. And the girl. New. Innocent. A surge of jealousy flooded its borrowed veins. Allan ignored her for the girl.

The old huntress, all sinew and leathery skin, shouted again, arguing with Allan while the girl—Morgan, that was her name—stood at her side, face pale and tight.

Cold pricked its skin, and it shivered until the gentle warmth of the flames washed over its body. It flexed its fingers, inhaling the wood smoke and scent of evergreen. Oh, to have weight and substance again. To be more than a breath of air. To be able to touch. To feel.

To eat.

***

Morgan shook Hanna's shoulder as she stared off into the dark, eyes glazing over and face going slack. It was almost as if she'd fallen into a trance. *What's wrong with her?* "Hanna? Are you okay?"

Hanna's fingers curled and uncurled. She blinked unevenly, but then her head snapped toward the old woman, a feral gleam in her eyes. She lunged at the woman, knocking her onto her back with a loud "Oof."

"Hanna!" Morgan raced to help Allan pry Hanna off the old woman.

Hanna tore at the woman's clothing, grabbing her scrawny hand when the woman went for the rifle still slung across her back. The woman cried out as Hanna caught her hand and squeezed.

Morgan's heart raced. *Oh God, Hanna, no! Have you lost your mind?*

Allan pulled Hanna off the woman and dragged her away. "What's wrong with you?"

Hanna shrieked and writhed in his arms, eyes bulging and wild.

"Help me with her!" Allan shouted, voice cracking.

Morgan grabbed at Hanna's legs but missed. A foot smashed against her nose. She fell back. Sharp pain lanced the back of her skull, radiating down her spine. Pain spread through her cheeks, mouth filling with blood. Her vision blurred, the fire before her morphing into a blob of light, blending with the darkness.

Someone yelled. Allan.

Everything went black.

***

The pulsing headache behind Morgan's eyes and an aching face and neck woke her. She brought a hand up to her nose, wincing. The skin was swollen and hot, the bridge crooked, but she could still breathe. *Broken, probably.* She'd expected there to be blood, too, but strangely, there was none. Her brain struggled to come up with a satisfying answer.

Beneath her was something soft and warm. *Blankets?* She opened her eyes and blinked, vision blurry. There was a bright, shifting light nearby. A fire, she thought, because of the comforting heat it gave off, but all the other objects were fuzzy.

A large, dark shape shifted in the corner of her eye. She sat up, head spinning, only to groan and fall back. She clamped a hand down on her mouth when burning acid crept up her throat.

"Calm down, girl. It's only me." Morgan knew that voice. The old woman from earlier. The one who had dealt with the deer and invaded their camp.

A blurry figure sat at a table nearby. At least, she thought it was a table; the details of everything were still smudged or haloed at the edges. When Morgan's vision finally sharpened a couple minutes later, she swung her legs around, planting her feet firmly on the floorboards before she carefully sat up.

The old woman tossed a small medicine bottle onto the cushion next to her. "You'll want to take a couple of those. I did the best I could, but I'm not a doctor."

The room was tiny but pleasantly warm with a crackling fire in the nearby hearth. The place reminded her of one of those old pioneer log cabins she'd seen in history books, cramped and lonely. "Where are we?"

"My home." The old woman lifted a steaming mug to her thin lips, drinking for a long moment before setting it back down with a dull thump. She kept her bandaged hand on the table, the fingers swollen and bruised. "Couldn't let that thing get you. You'll be safe here, it can't venture out this far."

"Thing?" Worms writhed in Morgan's belly. Allan. Hanna. They weren't here. What had happened? "Where are my friends?"

The woman's frown lines deepened. "Back at the underpass. The boy's fate has already been sealed. As for the girl...the beast has a hold on her until morning."

Morgan gripped the edge of the lumpy cushions beneath her. "No, you've got this all wrong. Hanna was just being dramatic. She was just trying to scare me." *Maybe I'm still unconscious or having a nightmare. That story couldn't be real...could it?*

The old woman shook her head. "That wasn't her; it was the creature. You're lucky I decided to check the underpass when I did. It's weak when it first takes hold, but it won't be once it feeds."

Morgan winced; maybe she'd hit her head harder than she'd thought. She took a couple of aspirin, dry swallowing them. "This is a joke, right? That story, it's just a town legend. Something to—"

"Do I look like a comedian?" The old woman's scowl deepened. "That thing is real. Do you really think your friend would go insane like that?"

"Well…no, but—"

"Then what more proof do you need?"

Morgan groaned, her skull pounding. *How did I get myself into this mess?* "Okay, fine, let's say I believe you. There has to be some way to free Hanna from whatever's possessing her and rescue Allan. It has to have a weakness. We could exploit it and—"

The old woman let out a short, harsh laugh. "You don't get it, do you? The only way to get rid of it is to kill Hanna. We're staying put until the sun's risen, and that thing has left her body. It *wants* us to go out there. Probably even planning for it. Either way, one of them will die."

"But Allan…we can't just leave him. Hanna will—if the legend's true—" *Hanna will eat him.* She failed to repress a shudder, her imagination conjuring up an image of Hanna bent over Allan's mangled body, a bloody heart clutched in her hand.

The old woman's face darkened, shadows from the fire playing across her weathered features. "There's nothing we can do for him. She's probably killed him by now. No point in risking your life as well."

"What if we called the police?" Morgan suggested. "They could do something, couldn't they?"

"Have you tried making a call out here? It's a dead zone. You'd never get ahold of them in time, and if by some miracle you did, she'd just kill whoever came by. They'd be dead before they even knew what they were walking into."

Morgan racked her brain. There had to be something…some way… "What about us? We could save them."

The old woman sighed, her wiry frame sagging against the curved back of the chair. Her crooked fingers trailed over her bandaged wrist before she met Morgan's gaze. "You haven't been listening. There's no point."

Morgan clenched her fists, nails biting in her palms. "You can't know that."

"Oh, but I do." The woman's eyes narrowed. She motioned to a frosted, moonlit window. "You think you're the first group to be attacked? This thing is ancient. Believe me, as long as there have been people out in these woods, it has fed on them."

"The solstice." A realization crept over Morgan like a shadow. Hanna hadn't mentioned anything about that. *Because she didn't know.* "You warned me when we met. You *knew* it would be out there tonight. How?"

"Local legend," the woman murmured with a shrug. "It doesn't matter."

"My friend, she said a group of teens went out there fifty years ago on a night like this…you…you were there…weren't you? You're *her*. The one that survived."

The old woman stared into the hearth, flames dancing across her eyes like molten sunlight. "All I know is it wants to gorge itself on every living thing that comes across its path."

Morgan's mouth went dry. She licked her cracked lips and finally spoke in a quiet voice. "What happens if we wait until morning?"

The old woman sighed. "It only gets the one night— the winter solstice. After that, the spell takes effect again, and it's banished until the next one."

Morgan nodded, a knot of regret forming in her throat. She had to do something if there was still a chance at saving Allan and Hanna. She couldn't just leave them to die; it wasn't right. "If you don't want to go with me, that's fine, but I can't stay here."

The woman eyed her. "That thing will kill you before you even get close to the underpass."

Morgan tried not to let her limbs shake as she stood and squared her shoulders. Her heartbeat pounded in her ears. "Do you have anything I can use? Your rifle, maybe?"

One of the woman's sparse eyebrows rose. "Do you even know how to use one?"

"Well, no, but—"

"Aw, hell." The woman groaned and shook her head. "You're going to be the death of me, aren't you?"

"Does this mean you'll come?" *Please say yes. I can't do this alone.*

The old woman's wrinkled mouth became a hard line. "If she's already killed the boy, she won't let us leave the underpass alive. I'll have to take her out."

Morgan's lip trembled. "Agreed."

"And you have to do everything I ask, even if you don't want to." The old woman rose from her chair, joints cracking. "It may look and act like your friend, but it's not. If it thinks it can trick you, it will. Are we clear?"

Morgan swallowed her rising doubts. If it meant a chance to save even one of them, she would take it. "Crystal."

***

In the quiet darkness of the tunnel, it crouched by Allan's body, head cocked as it watched the gentle rise and fall of his chest. Slowly, it closed its eyes, listening to the steady thrum of blood pumping through his veins. Such a lovely sound.

It reached toward his chest but recoiled at the sudden flash of pain arcing through its arm like a bolt of lightning. A hiss escaped its teeth. Gingerly, it cupped the deep slash across its bicep.

Fool.

It had been too eager to regain a physical form, and while it was still acclimatizing to its host, the old huntress had managed to injure it and drag the girl away. Only death or morning's light could part it from its host now.

Patience.

They would come for Allan. No matter their color or creed, humans were as predictable as the changing of the seasons, as brave as they were stupid. And if by some chance they didn't, then it would feast on the boy.

It stood and walked to the mouth of the tunnel to peer out at the blanket of stars in the blue-black sky.

A low growl rumbled in its throat. Just one night, that was all it had now. Such a pitiful existence.

Allan groaned softly. He turned over, barely visible in the smothering darkness, exposing the gash where it had cracked his head against the concrete road.

It settled down beside him, tracing one of the half-dried lines of blood trailing along his jaw and down his neck.

"Shh," it cooed. "They'll be here soon."

***

Morgan shut the pickup door with a soft click, her gaze going to Allan's nearby parked car. Her heart squeezed as she wrapped her fingers around the cold cross around her neck. She forced her quickening breath to slow, inhaling deeply before releasing it in a steady, opaque mist. *Please be alive.*

"Come on, we don't have time to waste," said the old woman gruffly.

"You're sure it'll be in the tunnel?" Morgan glanced at the darkness beyond the trees ahead. "How long have you been doing this? How many other people has it taken?"

"Are you always this talkative?"

"Not usually. I just—the more I know, the better I can be prepared…right?"

The old woman sighed, her voice tired. "The story your friend told you…that was the last time it fed. I've been able to drive off the others before nightfall…until you."

Morgan's gut churned uncomfortably. "How've you avoided being possessed all these years?"

"Because I'm smart enough to stay out of its range at night." The woman nodded to the path ahead. "Keep your eyes peeled and shout if you spot it."

Morgan gripped her heavy flashlight. *It. Not Hanna.* She had to remember that. "Hanna… What's going to happen to her?"

"What do you mean?" The old woman stalked ahead of her through a knee-deep section of snow, one of her hands on the holster at her side. With a small click, she drew the pistol.

"If that thing's inside her, is Hanna still there too?" She hadn't thought about it back at the cabin, more concerned about getting the woman to help her, but now that they were out here again, it crossed her mind.

"Yes, but she's buried deep. That thing, when it takes over…" The old woman's voice grew quiet. "It turns you into a flesh puppet. You have no control, but you're aware of everything that's happening."

"Oh my God, that's awful." *How would you even live with yourself afterward?*

"Enough questions," the woman snapped. "We need to listen."

Morgan sucked in a breath and trekked after the woman, tracing her footsteps. The underpass was only a few hundred feet from where they'd parked but far enough off the main road that, without a bonfire going, no one would be able to spot them if they ran into trouble.

A branch snapped off to Morgan's right.

She whirled toward the sound but saw only the faint outline of trees amid the darkness.

"Steady," said the old woman, lifting the gun.

"But what if it's Allan?" Morgan whispered. "Maybe he—"

"It's not. It's messing with your head. Trying to trick you," said the old woman harshly. "We keep moving."

Morgan's confidence wavered, but she nodded. *She knows this thing; I don't. Maybe I should listen.* The woman had refused to give her a weapon, deciding she was more likely to injure herself than be able to use it for self-defense. If the thing attacked her, she might be able to use her flashlight as a club, but that was it, unless the old woman intervened in time. *I hate being the bait...*

More branches cracked. Morgan startled. She paused, trying to determine direction.

"Keep up," snapped the old woman.

They kept walking. Morgan sensed eyes on her in the darkness. Wave after wave of goosebumps prickled her arms.

The fire at the entrance of the tunnel had been snuffed out, snow covering the ashy branches and logs they'd used to keep warm mere hours ago. A trail of bloody drag marks led into the underpass.

Morgan gripped her flashlight so hard her fingers throbbed.

The woods went silent again and the old woman halted, gun raised.

"What do we do?" asked Morgan in a shaky voice.

The woman pointed up at the sloping hill above the entrance to the underpass. "Check up there."

Morgan hesitated but did as she was told, shining her light above the tunnel's mouth. Just a few skeletal trees amid the snow. "It's clear."

The old woman turned, eyeing the forest beyond them. "Okay. Walk into the tunnel. I've got your back."

Morgan sucked in a lungful of cold air. *You can do this... This is why you're here. Please don't be a trap.* She shined her flashlight down the underpass and squinted. There was a dark shape in the distance, but she couldn't tell what it was.

It was big enough to be a person. Big enough to be Hanna or Allan. A chill seeped into her bones. "I-I see something."

"Is it moving?"

"No."

"Then keep walking. Carefully."

Morgan's guts twisted, but she did as the woman said, boots scuffing and scraping against the icy stretch of concrete. Her heart almost stopped when she finally was able to make out the figure. "It's Allan!"

He lay stretched out on his side at the center of the tunnel, his back to her. She let out a breath. He was okay!

"Damn lucky," said the old woman, sounding relieved. "Go check him."

Morgan ran and knelt beside him. Blood matted his hair and ran down his face near his ear, but he didn't seem to have any other injuries. *Just unconscious.* "Allan!"

She shook his arm, and he fell onto his back.

His chest had been cracked open, insides scooped out. Just a hollow shell.

Morgan screamed.

It was only when the sound died away that she could hear the inhuman cackling echoing off the walls.

Morgan's quivering hands clamped down over her mouth. Too late. They were too late.

The old woman grabbed her shoulder and yanked her to her feet. "We need to leave."

More cackling came from behind them.

Morgan spun, flashlight illuminating more empty road.

"Hanna! We know you're here! Come out!" shouted the old woman. She pointed to the end of the tunnel they'd come from. "Go. Get to the truck. I'll keep it off your back."

Morgan raced toward the tunnel's end, boots pounding against pavement.

Something swooped down on her at the tunnel mouth, crushing her to the ground. Pain lanced her body.

She swung her flashlight, the metal hitting flesh. The pressure lightened.

A gunshot cracked through the night. A monstrous scream rang out.

Something darted off into the woods, loping on all fours. Something that looked a great deal like Hanna.

The old woman helped Morgan to her feet. "We have to go after her."

Morgan bit down on her lip, hot tears streaming down her face. "But Hanna…she'll be free in the morning, won't she? What if—"

"No, she'll hunt us down. We'd never make it to the truck." The old woman pointed to the fresh blood trail ahead of them. "Follow it."

Faint crying met their ears.

With shaky legs, she followed the blood.

The crying grew louder.

Morgan aimed her flashlight between a couple of trees in the distance. "Hanna?"

Hanna crouched on her haunches, face clutched in her bloody hands. She sniffled. "Morgan?"

The old woman raised her weapon.

"Wait! Wait!" She stepped between Hanna and the old woman.

"Move." The old woman didn't lower her gun. "You said you would listen."

"But Hanna's still in there! You'd be murdering her, not that thing," said Morgan in a firm voice.

The old woman's fierce gaze flitted between Hanna and Morgan. "It's a trick."

"But what if it's not?" asked Morgan.

"She ate her brother. Do you know what it's like to live with that knowledge? Death is mercy." The old woman pushed past Morgan when she didn't move, raising her gun to Hanna's forehead. "Let me see your eyes."

Slowly, Hanna's hands came down. Her eyes shone with tears, and blood seeped from a bullet wound below her ribs. She pressed her hands against the wound and retreated, fear in her eyes. "Kill me. Please. It won't stop."

The woman pressed the gun barrel to Hanna's forehead, and she whimpered.

"Allan…" Hanna's voice trembled. "I… I…" She buried her face in her hands.

Morgan took a step forward. "Don't, please. This isn't right."

The old woman didn't budge. "Would you rather let her die of that wound or hypothermia then? At least this way it's quick."

Hanna's weeping turned to mocking laughter. "Don't kill me, please. Don't!"

Another gunshot cracked through the night.

Hanna slumped to the ground.

Morgan collapsed onto her knees, hands clamping down on her mouth. Her flashlight rolled a couple of feet away to shine on Hanna's limp body sprawled out like some grotesque ragdoll. "They're gone. They're both gone." She sobbed violently, body heaving and lungs unable to catch enough air. "This is all my fault."

The woman stayed silent, unmoving.

"Say something!" Morgan screamed, her voice going hoarse. She punched the ground when the woman still said nothing.

The fingers on the woman's good hand twitched. "Thank you."

Morgan blinked, gut clenching. "What?"

The old woman turned to her slowly; eyes blazing with that same feral quality she'd seen in Hanna's earlier. "That body was dying, and I needed another."

Morgan fell back. "No…" *No! No! No! It can't be!*

"Hush," the old woman tutted. She descended upon Morgan with superhuman speed, cutting her scream short. "You're mine now."

***

It sank back on its haunches, fat and happy as it watched the lightening horizon. It had minutes at most, but what a night it had been. Three kills. A feast after so many years of famine.

It swallowed down the rest of the girl's heart, licking its lips. It had done well to save her for last. Such sweet meat. It stroked her lovely red hair with bloody fingers. The girl's head lolled with each movement, her clouded eyes staring off into the distance.

As the first rays of light raced across the ground, the ancient spell's magic ripped it free from the old huntress's mind and body. Banished, it fled into the shadows once again.

The huntress collapsed into the snow and let out an agonizing, wounded scream, one of deep pain it had heard once long ago.

It slunk off into an abandoned rabbit burrow, nestling in the earth, ready to sleep for another year until the magic woke it again.

43 Market Street

Matthew Dewar

A severe storm warning had been broadcast on the television and radio all day. The eight residents of 43 Market Street had heeded the advice to stay inside their high-end apartment building, where they would be safe.

***

My eyes adjust to the dimness of her bedroom, and I follow the sounds and shape of her sleeping form.

Jumping on top of her, my knees pin her arms to the mattress, and I cover her mouth.

Eyes widen in shock. She strains against me. Her scream is muffled by my gloved hand.

I wave the large chef's knife I stole from her kitchen in front of her face then place it against my lips. "Shhh." Leaning down next to her ear, I inhale the warm, flowery scent of her hair. "Sweet dreams," I whisper.

Tears stream down her face.

The bedroom door cracks open, and every muscle in my body tenses. Holding my breath, I push down on her jaw with everything I have, muffling any potential cry for help.

With immense relief, the door closes again, and I relax.

My skin tingles in anticipation. My breathing quickens. The knife sinks deep into the soft flesh of her neck. There's a little resistance from her muscles and cartilage, but they give with a little more pressure.

Spurts of gurgling blood splatter across the room, peppering me with spray.

One down. Seven to go.

***

Trevor Nichols gingerly opened his bedroom door and reached behind it, fumbling in the dark for his coat. He left the light off, not wanting to wake his sleeping wife, who had just returned from a double shift at the hospital. She needed her six hours of uninterrupted sleep before returning for another double.

He hated how little time they spent together with the increasing demands of her medical fellowship and the long hours he had devoted to his case. He closed the door softly behind him and let her rest.

The windows in their living room rattled as the storm raged on outside. It was wilder than predicted. With a tink, the lights went out before blinking back on. His phone still had no reception. Pulling on his coat, he exited their apartment in search of a signal.

Trevor took the elevator down to the ground floor and followed the tiled hallway past the gym and indoor pool out to the back garden, where gale-force winds threatened to snap trees in half. Even waving his phone in the air didn't help pick up a signal.

He yelled into the howling wind, adding his rage and frustration to Mother Nature's fury. He should be at the station, interrogating his suspect. The Black Ravens were out there, destroying evidence and burrowing deeper underground. After arresting a high-ranking Black Raven gang member, his partner had been shot, and Trevor was suspended pending investigation.

"It wasn't my fault!" He kicked over a potted plant. "It wasn't." His last words were a pitiful whimper.

He could still feel Frank's body going limp in his arms as he bled out, and his sergeant's words echoing in his mind until he believed them. "Frank's death is on you. You're obsessed…going crazy…give me your badge…suspended until you pass a psych eval…"

No one believed him about the Black Ravens. As if he had concocted the country's biggest crime family in his head. "That's why you haven't heard of them," he growled. "They're the masterminds behind *everything*."

Trevor couldn't sit around doing nothing. His partner had made the ultimate sacrifice trying to put the Ravens away, and if he didn't do something about it soon, it would have been for nothing.

***

Steam rises from the surface of the spa.

Her robe falls to the ground in a pool of white fabric. She steps out of it with long, tanned legs as if she's performing for an audience.

She folds herself in half to untie the straps on her sandals.

I tiptoe up behind her. I could have some fun with her first, but I don't.

I wrap my gloved left hand around her head, drawing a surprised gasp from her lips. Pulling her head backward, I slice deeply across the front of her neck. Blood gushes from her golden skin like a crimson waterfall.

A flash of silver as the knife swings down in an arc and embeds itself deep into her chest between her ribs.

Her body falls limp. I drop her to the ground with a wet thud.

Two down.

***

Lily O'Dare padded through to the indoor swimming pool with an apologetic cocktail in each hand. Her soft flip-flops whispered against the tiles as she walked. Juggling the two glasses, she opened the door. Warm, humid air greeted her with the heaviness of chlorine. She spied the back of her daughter's head over in the spa.

Walking around the pool toward her, Lily took a sip of her drink and grimaced at its strength. It burned a little on the way down. "Hey, Hannah. Sorry I took so long. I decided to make us Long Island iced teas. Just what the doctor ordered."

Hannah didn't respond.

Lily continued to walk toward her. "Come on. You can't still be mad at me for—" The glasses shattered on the tiled floor as Lily's scream pierced the night. Her trembling hands covered her open mouth.

The spa water had turned a deep maroon, and the hilt of a kitchen knife protruded from Hannah's chest. Pale, open eyes stared vacantly into nothing.

"Hannah! Hannah! Wake up!" Lily screamed again, falling to her hands and knees. "Help!" She wailed until her voice went hoarse.

She retreated, pressing her back up against the cool wall. Tucking her knees to her chest, she closed her eyes and buried her face into her arms, but the image of her dead daughter remained etched into her mind.

****

Mary Mayweather couldn't contain her excitement at the sound of shrill shrieks echoing from downstairs. Gossip was her main source of currency, and it sounded like Lily and Hannah O'Dare from the apartment above hers were having another row.

Titillated by the prospect of watching the mother-daughter pair fight for the umpteenth time, Mary made her way downstairs at breakneck speed, despite the arthritic ache in her knees from the storm.

She beheld the scene before her with a mixture of horror and morbid curiosity. She couldn't wait to tell the ladies at bridge on Tuesday night what happened.

Mary hustled over to the distraught Lily and placed a hand on her shoulder. "Oh, Lily. Heavens above. Come with me, dear, and I'll set us a pot of tea." Mary licked her thumb and wiped a spot of dirt off Lily's white maxi dress. "Careful, dear, you're ruining your beautiful outfit."

"Call police," Lily mumbled.

"Oh no, dear. If there's one thing I learned from my previous marriages, we do not want to be calling the police when we're in a state. Sometimes we can let little words slip." She winked. "Let's calm you down and get your story straight before we do anything like that."

***

The world crushed in on Lily like a garbage compactor. All color and joy bled out of her surroundings until she was left with a depressing carcass of a life she didn't want to be a part of anymore.

A presence beside her reached for her, tried to help her up, to get her to go somewhere, to leave her daughter. She wouldn't. Couldn't.

Her Hannah. Her beautiful, smart, young Hannah was gone.

Light glinted off the edge of the knife still protruding from her baby's chest. If she could just reach it, she could be with her daughter again.

***

Upstairs, in apartment 2-B, opposite Hannah and Lily O'Dare in 2-A, Rebecca had finally managed to get little baby Austin to sleep when a piercing scream startled him awake again. With a wailing Austin on her shoulder, Rebecca shushed and patted him throughout the three-bedroom unit, searching for her husband. Sick little Austin needed his sleep, and her lazy husband could get off his lazy butt and help for once.

***

Harry smacked the side of the computer. "Come on!" Thanks to the storm, the Wi-Fi had failed, and the dancing naked girl had been replaced by an error popup. The study door opened, and his wife entered in sweatpants and a tank top stained with baby vomit.

Rebecca glared at him. "Will you go downstairs and see what's going on?" She started to walk out of the room before turning around with the wrath of a thousand scorned women. "You know what. I can't take this anymore. You tell Lily that Hannah needs to move out. I can't stand the drama. Either she goes, or we do." And with that, she stormed out of the room.

"Okay." Harry stared after his wife, now relieved the internet went down. She had never quite recovered after her pregnancy. It was as if he didn't exist unless she needed something from him, like a diaper changed or a load of laundry hung up. He cleared his browser history and turned the computer off. Barefoot, in loose gray track pants and a white t-shirt, he left the apartment, cursing as their cat appeared out of nowhere and darted out the open door. She would be back, scratching on the door soon enough. Sighing, Harry jogged down the fire escape to investigate a noise he didn't even hear.

***

They don't know I'm here.
They can't see me...
...but I can see them.

***

Trevor was walking back toward the elevator when Harry burst out the door to the stairwell, muttering a creative string of curse words under his breath. Trevor acknowledged Harry with a nod.

"The hell's going on down here?" Harry asked.

"What?"

"The screaming? You didn't hear it either?" Harry glanced around.

"Nah, I was outside trying to make a call. Stupid storm. Does your phone have reception?"

Harry shrugged. "Dunno. Left it upstairs. Becca's gone crazy up there though. Lily and Hannah are fighting again, apparently. She says she wants to move out."

"Will you?" Trevor followed Harry's eyes to the door leading into the pool where Mary had appeared. She beckoned them over.

Mary threw open the door for them, and Trevor could tell something was wrong. The strong chlorine smell was mixed with something coppery.

Mary pointed to Lily. "I tried to get her to move, but she won't leave." In a lower voice, she added, "I think she killed Hannah. Accidentally. Probably." She poked Trevor in the chest. "You need to do something."

Harry hung back, looking green as Trevor approached Hannah's body. Mary followed him like an eager toddler.

Following several deep breaths and groans, Harry threw up behind them. Trevor stifled a smirk. After nearly a decade working as a policeman, and another as a detective, there wasn't much that Trevor hadn't seen. Mary was right to think Lily had done it, but he knew better. He clenched his jaw. The Ravens. They were here for him. Hannah had probably seen them, and they had killed her.

The walls of the apartment shook with a deafening boom of thunder, and the lights flickered again.

"Hey, Harry. Take Lily back to Mary's. I'm going to check the scene and call this in."

"Good idea." Mary nodded enthusiastically. "Do you think the police will want something when they get here? Do I have time to bake a cake? Or will cookies do?"

Trevor shook his head. The sooner he was alone, the better. The Ravens were probably here. Watching him right now. Waiting to get him alone so they could kill him. He would end this. Now. Before another death strangled his conscience.

***

They're scared.
They should be.
I'm just warming up.

***

With a sniveling Lily lying on one of the plastic-protected floral sofas, Mary set a pot of water on the stove. Her curly white hair swished as she faced the man in her living room.

"What happened?" Harry asked, pacing the room. "Did Lily…?"

"I think so." Mary waved a hand in Lily's direction. "Look at her. I haven't been able to get any sense out of her." She cocked her head. "I wonder if I should get out a photo of my granddaughter, in case there are any good-looking single policemen." She turned her attention back to the whistling pot of water.

Harry rubbed his hands across his face. "Are you okay looking after Lily? I'm going to go and check on Becca and Austin."

Mary spun around and nodded enthusiastically.

***

Harry's bare feet slap against the concrete steps as he runs up them two at a time.

Completely unaware of me behind him.

He slows down at the top, breathing heavy.

Before he can open the door, I pull back on his shoulders.

Down! Down! Down he goes! Limbs flailing.

His head hits the concrete platform at the bottom of the stairwell, and he grunts.

His eyes open in fear as I descend upon him.

I grab his head in my hands and pound it against the floor until the thuds give way to a squelching sound. I inhale deeply, basking in the rapture of my conquest.

Three down.

***

Trevor ignored Hannah's dead body. He knew Ravens didn't leave any evidence behind. One was here. Waiting to get him alone so they could end him. Probably kidnap and torture him first. But the pool was empty. The pump room deserted. Every nook and cranny devoid of any suspicious persons.

Even with his life in jeopardy, there was no way he was calling the police. It's not like he could anyway with no service. Not when it had everything to do with the Black Ravens. And especially since nobody believed him. This was his battle, and he would not give up easily. With his badge and gun suspended, he was free to seek his vengeance.

Confident the area was safe from immediate threat, he took a moment to examine Hannah's body. The knife in her chest was the same brand he had back in his apartment. It was a popular set that Breeana had bought last Christmas, and Trevor wondered how many other thousands of people had purchased it. Too hard to trace.

A small dent on the handle caught his attention. He remembered the day Breeana dropped the knife, nearly cutting off her toe. Luckily, she was fine. The only damage was a small dent. He swore under his breath. The Black Ravens had framed him. They were here. *They had been in his apartment.*

He pulled the knife from her chest and cleaned it quickly before rushing to the elevator. They were framing him. Someone had broken into his apartment to steal the knife. The same apartment where his wife was fast asleep, unprotected. They weren't here to kill him. They were here to completely discredit him and frame him for murder.

His heart thundered in his chest as he raced to his apartment and stood outside their bedroom door. He opened it with a heavy heart and strained to hear, but there was no soft breathing of a sleeping woman.

With a sickening feeling in his gut, his nostrils identified a familiar smell.

His hand hovered over the light switch, not wanting to confirm what his gut already knew.

He flicked on the lights.

Breeana lay in a pool of blood. A deep gash cut across her throat.

Thick blood dripped down the wall, coming from the words: "You should have turned on the lights."

A guttural cry drained Trevor's lungs, fueling his anguish. He punched the door hard. Wood splintered and cracked, and his knuckles burned with searing pain. He swore. Gripping the knife tighter in his hand, he scanned the apartment for any signs of an intruder.

Bloodlust tightly gripped Trevor's mind, and he vowed to never sleep until every last Black Raven was rotting in the ground. A quick death would be a luxury they would not experience.

Walking out into the foyer, he waited for the elevator. The doors opened and he raised his knife high at the sight of the woman inside.

Rebecca screamed, clutching a white baby monitor in front of her face.

"I'm so sorry," he said, quickly holding his hands up, pointing the knife away from her. Despite his apology, he couldn't help but wonder who Rebecca and Harry really were. Could they be Ravens themselves? Or at least working for them? His mind raced with paranoia. How well did he really know anyone?

"What the hell, Trevor?" She took several steadying breaths. "You scared me half to death!"

Trevor clutched the knife tightly, willing his trembling hands to still. "Sorry. I'll explain in a minute."

"Where's Harry? He hasn't come back yet." A rustling sound crackled over the baby monitor, and Rebecca pressed her ear against it to listen.

"He's downstairs in Mary's apartment. I'm headed there now." Trevor stood in silence until the elevator reached the first floor, and the doors opened out onto the landing. "Hannah's dead." He carefully studied her reaction.

Rebecca froze mid-step. She clutched the baby monitor tightly in her left hand and her right hand rested against her chest. "What? What happened? Is Austin safe?"

"Austin is fine. You can hear him on the monitor. Let's go find Harry and sort this mess out." Trevor led the way to Mary's front door.

***

Rebecca and Trevor entered Mary's apartment to a dining room table laden with steaming cups of black tea in fine china, a plate of shortbread cookies, and a milk jug next to a saucer of sugar cubes.

Mary glanced up with a beaming smile, but her face fell. "Oh, it's just you two. Are the police on their way?"

Trevor nodded. "There are delays because of the storm, but they'll get here as fast as they can." There was no point in adding more panic than necessary. He had it under control. The police were unnecessary. "Is Harry here?"

Mary shook her head. "No, he left a few minutes ago to check on Rebecca and Austin."

Rebecca sighed. "We must have just missed him. He never takes the elevator, especially not in a storm."

"Mind if I use the bathroom?" Trevor asked.

Mary nodded. "Of course. That'll give me the chance to fill Rebecca in on what she's missed." She licked her lips as she glanced over to the whimpering Lily on her sofa. "Come, sit down. Do you take milk and sugar with your tea?"

"What?" Austin stirred on the baby monitor, and Rebecca turned up the volume to maximum. The storm continued to howl outside. "Trevor said Hannah's dead." She glanced over at Lily on the couch, whose face was buried into a cushion, sobbing. She didn't know whether to leave her be, or go and console her. Her world would be over if anything happened to Austin.

The corners of Mary's lips twitched up into a smile. "Oh yes. And I think we know who did it." She surreptitiously pointed toward Lily with a knowing nod.

With a shaky hand, Rebecca brought her black tea to her lips and blew gently before taking a small sip. Her stomach churned. A mother could never harm their child. Ever. She was tempted to rush back up to her apartment and squeeze Austin tightly. If he wasn't sick and needing sleep, she'd do exactly that.

Mary plopped three sugar cubes in her tea and stirred.

Trevor walked back into the room with a heavy sigh. "Your apartment's fine. I'm going to ask you all to stay here, together, and remain calm."

"Calm?" Rebecca demanded.

Trevor ignored the question and faced Mary. "Keep the door locked at all times. I'm going to bring Harry and Austin here and then catch the bastard who's responsible for this."

Mary gasped. "So it wasn't Lily?"

Trevor shook his head, sniffing and wiping his eyes. "The same thing happened to Breeana."

A bubbling cry escaped Rebecca's mouth. Her eyes widened as her knuckles whitened around the baby monitor. "I need to get Austin!"

"Oh my." Mary covered her mouth.

"You're safer here," Trevor said. "And Harry's probably with Austin right now. I'm going to get them now and bring them here." Without a backward glance, he sped out of Mary's apartment.

Rebecca shook her head. "I haven't seen Harry since he came down earlier. Where is he?" Her heart ached in her chest. Was he okay?

Mary held out the plate of shortbread cookies. "These will take your mind off everything."

Rebecca declined.

The baby monitor crackled with static. Austin's light breathing was joined with heavier breaths.

Rebecca's knuckles turned white as she gripped the edge of the table.

"See, Harry's checking on Austin. Everything's fine," Mary remarked.

"There, there, little guy. It's going to be all right," a voice that was not Harry's crackled with static.

Rebecca left Mary's apartment in a whirlwind, leaving a stunned Mary with her mouth hanging open.

***

The baby is a dead weight in my arms. So peaceful.

"There, there, little guy. It's going to be all right," I say, placing him back in his crib. His little chest rises and falls with his breaths. His face scrunches up, and he opens and closes his mouth several times.

A door bursts open and I retreat to the wardrobe.

It's not your time, little Austin.

Not yet.

***

Rebecca burst into Austin's room and raced to his crib. She glanced over her shoulder, sensing a shadow move to the wardrobe. "Harry?" No one was there. Her legs shook and threatened to collapse underneath her.

She let out a small cry of relief as she gazed down upon her sleeping son, alive and unharmed. "Thank God," she whimpered. "I don't know what I'd do if I lost—"

Intense pressure like she had never known constricted around her throat with crushing force. She slapped, kicked, punched, and tried to wriggle free, but her strength faded rapidly.

***

Mary sipped her tea, keenly listening to the baby monitor.

She listened to Rebecca whispering to Austin. She shifted forward in her seat as the words were cut out and replaced with strangled chokes.

***

So vulnerable. Weak. With firm pressure over her carotid arteries, it isn't long before death consumes her. She tries to break free with all the strength of a feather. Useless.

I maintain the pressure around her throat after her body goes flaccid, until I know for sure the life has faded from her. After several minutes, I drop her unceremoniously at the foot of Austin's crib.

Before leaving, I pause at a shelf to crank a music box several times. The twinkling sound fades as I go in search of my next victim.

Only three to go.

***

Trevor crashed through Mary's front door with a sleeping baby Austin resting against his shoulder. "They're dead," he managed through gasps.

Mary stood over the table with the baby monitor in her hands, head shaking slowly. "Harry, too?"

Eerie music box chimes came through the baby monitor.

Trevor nodded. "How's she doing?" Trevor inclined his head toward Lily, who remained on the couch, face buried in a pillow, body shaking with grief.

"No change. Tea?"

Trevor took a few deep breaths before sitting and accepting the offered tea with a cube of sugar and a dash of milk. "Thanks," he managed, swallowing the lump in his throat. He didn't understand what game the Black Ravens were playing. They had already framed him for murder; why did they need to kill everyone? Maybe he should have listened to his sergeant. Left it alone. If he hadn't been so determined to put them away, everyone would be fine. Breeana would still be alive.

"Earth to Trevor!" Mary waved a shortbread cookie in his face.

Trevor shook himself. "Sorry. What?"

"I said, what happened to Harry?" She broke the cookie in half and began munching on it.

Trevor took a long sip from his tea and set the cup down on its saucer. "I was heading upstairs when I found Harry dead at the bottom of the stairwell. His head..." Trevor turned his face to the floor. "There was so much blood."

The door slammed shut behind him.

Both Trevor and Mary jumped.

"Who's there?" Mary whispered.

Trevor stood and glanced around the room. No one had entered. But someone had left.

"Lily's gone."

***

Mary and Trevor waited an agonizing minute for the elevator. Mary's knees couldn't manage the stairs, and Trevor didn't want to leave her or Austin alone. The baby's head rested against his shoulder, occasionally smacking his lips. There was little he could do to quell the guilt rising and crushing his chest. It was his duty to serve and protect. But that duty had led to the death of his Breeana and their neighbors, and had left poor little Austin an orphan.

"We need to find Lily," Trevor said, clearing his voice to sound more confident than he felt. "Then we need to get the hell out of here."

Mary nodded. "Where do you think she's gone?"

"We'll check their apartment, then the pool."

The elevator chimed and the doors opened. Mary stepped inside and asked Trevor, "Do you have a gun?"

Trevor shook his head and waited impatiently for the doors to shut, pressing the "Close Doors" button repeatedly.

Mary pressed something cold and hard into his side.

Instinct kicked in and Trevor spun, twisting the gun out of Mary's hands and turning it on her.

Mary shrieked and threw her hands into the air. "Don't shoot me!"

"What the hell?" Trevor growled. "Where did you even get a gun from?"

"I was…passing it…to you." Mary clutched her chest and took in big gulps of air. "Young people like to prey on us oldies. I need to protect myself."

Austin stirred. His limbs stretched, and a grumble sounded on his lips. But he fell silent once more.

Trevor noticed the safety was still on. "Sorry. Old habits." He tucked the double-action revolver into the back of his pants. He peered into the bag hanging over her shoulder. "Got any other goodies in there?"

***

The elevator's soft music wrapped the three of them in awkward silence as they climbed.

"Do you think we're going to die?" Mary whispered. "I'm too young to die."

Trevor rested his free hand on her shoulder and stared into her eyes. "I will do everything in my power to protect you, even if you are delusional about your age." The confidence boost and joke seemed to lift Mary's spirits, but it didn't work on Trevor. He knew what he was up against, and the Black Ravens were nothing if not deadly.

Trevor checked his phone again. Still no reception, and all the landlines he had tried so far were all dead. His sergeant should've believed him. This all could have been prevented if he could have started the task force he needed to take them down.

The door to apartment 2-B was ajar. Soft music box music chimed from deep within the dark apartment. Mary followed Trevor to 2-A as fast as her arthritic knees could handle.

"Do you think we're dealing with one person or a team?" Mary asked as Trevor passed Austin to her. "Do you think they're still in the apartment? Why do you think they're killing us? Have they stolen anything? Are they looking for something?" She took in a breath. "Trevor, answer me!"

"Your guess is as good as mine."

At that moment, another huge gust of wind rattled the windows. The storm was picking up, and a boomclap of thunder later, the apartment building plunged into impenetrable darkness.

***

Holding Austin in one arm, Mary fumbled in her handbag for the flashlight she knew was inside. She felt her pepper spray, a tube of lipstick, her pack of menthol cigarettes, and then her small but powerful flashlight. She clicked it on, and a beam of light spilled across the landing.

She handed the flashlight to Trevor who adjusted his grip on her revolver. He proceeded carefully, ready for anything.

Spinning toward the sound of tapping against a window, Trevor relaxed. His light revealed a branch scratching the glass in the wild winds outside. His pulse pounded in his ears.

Lily's door was locked, and with no other way to enter, he kicked it in, wood splinters peppering the floor.

The beaming light swept over every room of the empty apartment, and when Trevor concluded that it was indeed deserted, they retreated downstairs to the pool.

***

Lily sat by the edge of the spa, stroking Hannah's hair. An endless stream of tears dampened her white dress. She squinted into the light as Trevor's flashlight pointed at her. He lowered it, and Mary walked around the pool to comfort Lily, still clutching Austin in her arms.

There was a loud crash inside the pump room, and Mary screamed. Austin woke and began to wail.

Trevor sprinted around to the two women and handed Mary the flashlight. "Take Lily and get out of here. I'll handle this."

Mary shook her head. "We'll be safer in my apartment. Lord knows what's outside."

Trevor watched them leave and allowed his eyes to adjust to the dark. An occasional flash of lightning illuminated the otherwise dark room.

***

Trevor took a deep breath in front of the pump room door and prepared himself for whatever was waiting for him on the other side. This was it. He was going to catch one of the Black Ravens. His sergeant would have no choice but to give him back his badge and gun and fund a task force to bring them down. He would deliver his vengeance on every last one of them.

With a splintering crash, he kicked the door open and pointed the gun into the dark room.

Large, angular shapes loomed around him, but nothing moved. He waited, holding his breath, finger hovering above the trigger.

A flash of lightning briefly lit up the space. The room was empty.

As the room plunged into darkness once more, the pool scooper crashed to the floor at his feet.

Trevor pulled the trigger on the revolver reflexively, and a deafening boom made his ears ring.

He leapt backward with a yell as a meowing cat pranced out of the room.

For a minute, Trevor just breathed.

But if the Black Raven wasn't here…

***

Mary brought Lily up to her apartment, locked the door, and set about lighting all the candles and oil lamps around her living and dining rooms. An aroma of vanilla and sandalwood lifted into the air.

"Can I use your toilet?" Lily murmured.

"Oh, of course, dear." Mary pointed to a white door down the hallway. "I'll boil the kettle."

Shadows danced around the room with the flickering light from the candles.

A gunshot rang out downstairs, and Mary cursed under her breath. She prayed Trevor was okay. She couldn't believe what had happened around her today. Her luck had turned. She would be retelling this story for years. But what happened to the police that Trevor had called earlier? Perhaps she should call to complain about their poor service. Her shortbread cookies were growing stale. She picked up the receiver, but the line was dead. "What are we going to do about this, Austin?"

The toilet flushed, and Mary jumped, forgetting for a moment that Lily was back there. She clutched Austin against her bosom.

Footsteps preceded a knock at the front door, and Mary's heart froze in her chest. Potential weapons were all around her, but she relaxed when she heard Trevor's voice.

"It's me."

She unlocked the door and let him in.

"You okay?" she asked. "I heard a shot. Did you get him?"

Trevor shook his head. "There was no one there. It was an accident."

A vacant Lily walked into the room and sat at the table.

"Here, dear. Let me do that for you." Mary poured a fresh cup of tea for Lily and handed it to her. "The phones are down," she said, glancing back at Trevor.

"I know. They've been down all night."

Mary's heart caught in her chest.

If the phones have been down all night, he never placed the call. Why would he lie about that? Unless…

Trevor.

He was the only one who'd been unaccounted for during each murder. He was the only one capable of killing people so effortlessly.

Mary hated leaving Lily alone with the murderer, but she had to prioritize her own safety. He had the gun, but she still had her late husband's pistol in the top drawer beside her bed.

Mary shivered. "It's freezing. I'm just going to go get a jacket." She toddled off to her room as fast as her legs could take her.

***

She walked right past me.

She has no idea how close she is to death.

I follow her as she places the baby on her bed and bends down to open the nightstand drawer.

I grab her head in my hands and twist her neck sharply. With a sickening crunch, her final breath leaves her, and I lower her onto the floor.

My fun's almost coming to an end.

The final two.

***

With a hum of electricity, the lights came back on. Trevor's phone still lacked service, but Mary's landline had a dial tone.

Calling his precinct, he tapped his foot impatiently as he waited for someone to answer. "Come on. Pick up. Pick up." Chewing on the inside of his cheek, he cursed himself for not calling this in earlier. He thought he had a handle on the situation, but clearly he didn't.

He could hear Mary shuffling about in her room. The sooner he made contact with someone, the sooner everyone would be safe.

"Good evenin—"

"It's me, Trevor Nichols. I need to speak to the Sarge right now. It's urgent."

"I'm sorry, Trevor, he doesn't want to talk to you." Her sweet voice was tainted with impatience.

"Put me through, now!" he growled.

"He told me not to disturb him tonight for anything."

"Just do it," he spat into the phone.

There was a brief pause, followed by a heavy sigh. "Okay, I'll patch you through to his cell. But no complaints if he doesn't answer."

A muffled buzz came from Mary's room, and he briefly wondered what she was up to. She was full of surprises, like the gun in the elevator. Hell, she was probably fetching a stick of dynamite. At this point, nothing would surprise him.

The dial tone clicked as his sergeant picked up. "Brian."

Trevor's shoulders relaxed. "It's me. Trevor. Look, you've got to believe me. The Black Ravens are real. They're in my apartment building. They've killed innocent people."

Trevor strained to hear a response. But there was nothing but muffled movements.

Brian finally answered in a quiet voice. "You better not be pulling a stunt. I'll send a patrol over and try to get there myself as fast as possible."

Trevor hung the phone back on the receiver before blowing out the now unnecessary candles and returning to the dining room table to sit beside Lily. "It's okay. The cops will be here soon."

Lily sniffed. "It's too late for Hannah though." As wracking sobs took over her body, Trevor took Lily into his arms and let her cry.

***

It wasn't long before there was a booming knock on Mary's door. "Trevor, open up. It's Brian."

Lily started as Trevor stood up to move. "It's okay. The police are here now."

Trevor opened up the door to find Brian in civilian clothes: dark jeans, a dry, black leather jacket, and black motorcycle gloves. "You better have something concrete. Tonight's been flat out with the storm, and I'm not in the mood for your Raven crap."

"Come in." Trevor poked his head out into the hallway. "Are the uniforms here yet?"

"They're on their way."

Trevor closed the door and led Brian through to the living room.

"So where are all these dead bodies you were talking about?" Brian asked with a sigh. "Any black feathers?"

"Strewn about the complex. And no feathers. They're framing me. I'm the only one who gives a damn about putting them away, and they're trying to get rid of me."

"Do you know how crazy you sound right now?"

Trevor shook his head. "It's all real. I promise you. Come up to my apartment, I'll show you Breeana's—hang on. Why did you come to this apartment and not mine?"

Brian frowned. "I went to your apartment, but no one was there. I knocked on every door until I found you."

"And why are you in civvie clothes? How did you get here so fast?" Trevor snapped his hand around to grab the gun from his jeans, but stopped dead in his tracks as a black muzzle was pointed at his face.

"Hands up," Brian ordered. "It's such a shame about your mental breakdown."

"What are you talking about?" he growled.

Brian jerked the gun, and Trevor began walking backward. "The breakdown that's been brewing for some time now. The obsession with a fictional crime ring. The risky behavior that led to the death of your partner and your suspension. Which all culminated in tonight. A massive psychosis that led you to believe your neighbors were Black Raven gang members. You killed every last one of them, before committing suicide."

Trevor stared into Brian's impassionate eyes. "How could you?" he snarled. "You killed Breeana!"

"And I'm not done yet." Brian raised an eyebrow. He pointed the gun at Lily and pulled the trigger.

Austin began wailing from Mary's room.

Trevor blinked away the flash while his ears rung. His hands flew through the air toward his gun. He needed to protect baby Austin.

"Hands back up," Brian barked.

Trevor's fists clenched. He was so close. "Brian. Please. You don't have to do this."

Spittle flew from Brian's mouth as he spoke. "Yes, I do. I tried to warn you off the Ravens. I practically begged you to stay away from them. But here we are. My hands are tied."

The windows rattled, and thunder exploded above them. The lights flickered twice but remained on.

"Why?" Trevor breathed heavy. "Why?"

Brian's eyes narrowed. "One favor. It started as one favor. Ten years ago, I accepted help from a gang member to put away one of their competition. I was an idiot. I owed them, and every time I thought I had paid my debt, they would blackmail me. They owned me." His face opened into a smile. "But after a while, it turned out to be the best mistake of my life. Crime really does pay. And they pay really well for me to keep them in the shadows."

With a second explosive thunderclap, the apartment plunged into darkness once more.

Trevor pulled the gun out of his pants and aimed at the outline of his sergeant.

***

A gunshot cracked louder than the thunder before it.

A body fell to the ground with a heavy thud.

The lone survivor aimed his gun in the direction of the rasping breathing. With one more shot, the breathing finally ceased.

***

Our secret has been preserved.
The Black Ravens will remain in the shadows.

***

43 Market Street appeared on television screens all across the country. Flashing police vehicles littered the street, and tape cordoned off the large crowd that had gathered despite the horrible weather. The hero of the night, Sergeant Brian Hannon, addressed the reporter with the sole survivor, a small baby, in his arms. "It was a terrifying ordeal, and the details are still being pieced together, but what I can say is that residents can rest assured that the perpetrator was shot and killed on the scene. Once again, your homes and families are safe."

Author Biographies

Louise Ross – The Cat Lady

Louise Ross is a writer from the greater Kansas City area. When not quilting and working, she lives in a fantasy world where ordinary creatures build everyday lives outside the major battles and politics.

"The Cat Lady" comes from a writing challenge. Originally written as a tragedy, it failed to have the impact Louise wanted. Turning the tragedy into a horror story allowed a exploration of consequences and a creature Louise has always been suspicious of, cats.

Check out Louise Ross on Facebook (@alouiseross), Twitter (@A_Louise_Ross), or her blog (83louross.wordpress.com).

Mckayla Eaton – The Lighthouse

Mckayla is an aspiring author of science fiction and fantasy. She's won three honorable mentions for three separate short stories submitted to Writers of the Future, an international science fiction and fantasy short story competition for amateur writers.

She lives in Halifax, Nova Scotia, Canada, and is going into the last year of her BA at the University of Kings College.

She's currently working on three fantasy novels, her main project being a young adult fantasy about a young wizard who has to go to Hell and back to defeat a dangerous demon.

You can find her on Instagram as @mckayla_schneider.

Melion Traverse – Beware the Autumn People

Melion Traverse is an elusive creature with a fondness for historical fencing (swords, not boundary markers), martial arts, weightlifting, and medieval Latin. Melion's works have appeared in publications such as *Deep Magic*, *Cast of Wonders*, *Cosmic Roots and Eldritch Shores*, and *Havok*.

The story "Beware the Autumn People" is a homage to the great Ray Bradbury whose wordcraft captivated a young Melion and still haunts her on autumn nights.

You can find more of Melion's writings at her blog (https://delusionsofsanityblog.wordpress.com/).

Hanna Day – The Renewal

Hanna Day is a writer from Southern California with an interest in history, fantasy, and the deep, dark existential horrors of the unknown. When not contemplating the vastness of space or writing, she works as a digital marketer.

"The Renewal" was inspired by the works of H. P. Lovecraft. Other publications include contributions to local newspapers and magazines.

Follow her ongoing existential crises on Twitter (@hannacday).

Maemi Mizunami – The Girl

Maemi Mizunami was raised on literature and fiction, and has always dreamed of being a published author. Her story, "The Girl," was inspired by a conversation with a friend's daughter. She loves dogs and laments that her apartment in Japan doesn't allow pets, otherwise she would have two or three of them.

You can follow her on Twitter (@maemi_mizunami).

Renée Harvey – Sargasso 1840

Renée Harvey is a wife and mother, historian and author in Idaho, USA. She writes about little-known people from the past with stories to share, as discovered in "Sargasso 1840".

Her other publications include "Daughter of the Air" in *From the Stories of Old*, and "I Choose" in *Between Heroes and Villains*.

Follow her research in medieval and Hopewell societies and novel progress on the Rochegude series and Hopewell Chronicles on Twitter and Facebook (@PRHarvey6) and at her blog (storytellerreneeharvey.wordpress.com).

Heather Hayden – In Her Reflection

Though a part-time editor by day, Heather Hayden's not-so-secret identity is that of a writer—at night she pours heart and soul into science fiction and fantasy novels. She is currently working on *Upgrade* (the sequel to her first published novel) and an as-yet-untitled series of fairy tale novelizations.

Heather has never written horror before, but she accepted the challenge with excitement. Her story, "In Her Reflection," was inspired by a nightmare she had years ago. She dedicates it to her friend Bartholomew Lander, whose spectacular series *The Warren Brood* convinced her that horror could be enjoyable.

You can follow Heather's writing adventures at her blog (www.hhaydenwriter.com) and on Twitter and Facebook (@HHaydenWriter). Her first novel, a young adult fiction story titled *Augment*, was published in 2015. She also has two short stories published: "Beneath His Skin," a retelling of the selkie myth, in *From the Stories of Old*, and "In A Breath," an original superpower story, in *Between Heroes and Villains*.

Cassandra Lee Yieng – Don't Offend a Girl in Love

Cassandra Lee Yieng loves to challenge the status quo. Being a writer, artist, musician, mathematician, and computer scientist, she enjoys breaking the barriers between art, science, and business. Because of her unusual background, she has written articles, given speeches, and tweeted on women in STEM (science, technology, engineering, and mathematics) and on how she is no typical "nerd". Based in Hong Kong, Cassandra has written for global publications and websites before joining the Just-Us League in January 2017. A teacher now, she inspires students to reach for the sky.

Her cybersecurity horror story, "Don't Offend A Girl In Love," is inspired by the single "Lately" written by Hong Kong independent musician Kirk Ng. You may learn more about Kirk through his Facebook page (@kirkngmusic). Other lyrical influences include "Scars" by Tove Lo and Regina Spektor's cover of "While My Guitar Gently Weeps" featured in the animated film *Kubo and the Two Strings*.

You can get in touch with Cassandra via her website (http://leeyieng.com), Facebook (@cassandraleeyieng), Instagram (@cassandraleeyieng), and Twitter (@leeyieng).

Katelyn Barbee – The Solstice Beast

Katelyn Barbee is a Phoenix college student by day and a writer by night. When not working on her fantasy series, you can find her at the cinema catching the latest flicks or enjoying a nature walk when the weather is nice.

The story "The Solstice Beast" was inspired by her love of horror movies and working in the wee hours before sunrise when her imagination is overactive and anything seems possible.

Her other publications include "The Miller's Daughter" in *From the Stories of Old*. You can connect with Katelyn on Twitter (@WriterBarbee) or on Facebook (katelyn.barbee.9).

Matthew Dewar – 43 Market Street

Matthew's passion for reading and writing developed at a young age. Fascinated by all genres, enthralled by the endless creativity of imagination, and captivated by foreign worlds and intriguing characters, Matthew makes time in his busy schedule to write every day. If he's not reading or writing, you might find Matthew working as a physiotherapist, teaching group fitness classes, entertaining his dog, or dreaming of traveling to an exotic destination.

In May 2017, Matthew published *Nightmare Stories*, a collection of young adult horror fiction where twelve young teens discover that happily ever afters only exist in fairy tales. His short stories have appeared in *From the Stories of Old*, *Between Heroes and Villains*, *The Seven Deadly Sins Anthology: Gluttony*, and *The Seven Deadly Sins Anthology: Wrath*.

You can connect with Matthew on Twitter (@WriterDewar), Facebook (Matthew Dewar Author), or at his website: matthewdewarauthor.wordpress.com.

About the Illustrator

Heidi Hayden was raised in the forests of Maine and graduated from the Maine College of Art as an Illustration major. A bookworm by nature, she reads copious amounts of questionable fiction by unpublished authors, in the few moments of spare time when she is not writing and illustrating her own books. She works in gouache, ink, pencil, and fabric, and enjoys repurposing materials for her art.

You can see more of her work on her website: haydenillustration.com.

About the Just-Us League

Hailing from all corners of the globe, the members of the Just-Us League share a common passion for words and worlds.

The League can be found on Facebook (@jlwriters), Twitter (@JL_writing), and our website (jlwriters.com). Follow us for updates, giveaways, and new releases.

Also by the Just-Us League

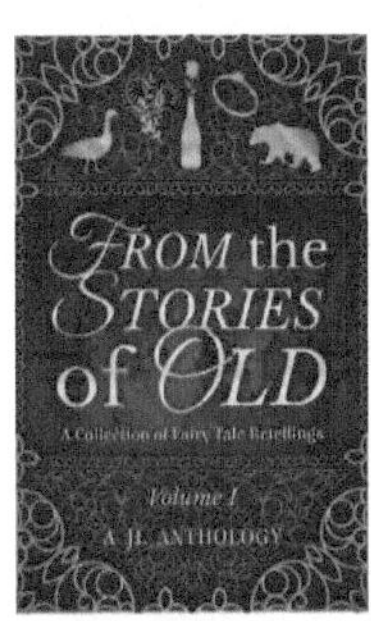

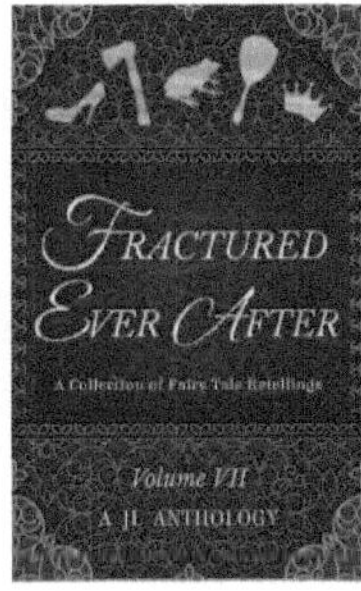